DARK
OF
NIGHT _{EPISODE 1}

CS DUFFY

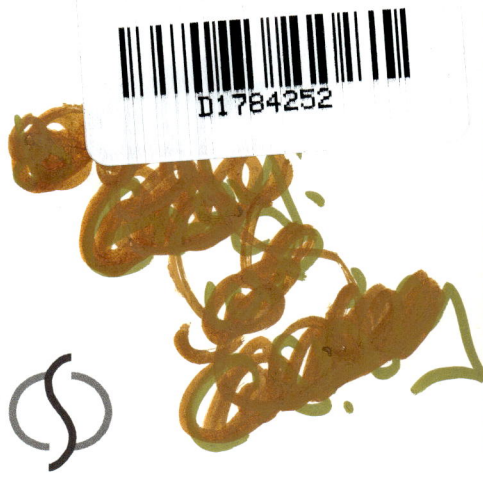

D1784252

PRAISE FOR C.S. DUFFY

I think Glasgow has just found itself a fresh new name in crime fiction! Dark of Night is short and sharp, full of the Glasgow banter and humour laced with a good old-fashioned murder mystery....The characters in the book are authentic "Glesga" characters with that dry wit, irreverent humour and that way of telling a stranger your life story if you stand beside them for longer than 5 minutes, shone throughout the book.

ChapterinMyLife Blog

...For all they are about a serial killer, there is a lot of humour in them too and a real sense of warmth towards Glasgow and its people. CS Duffy has created brilliant and very likeable characters in Ruari and Cara who both feel very authentic in their thoughts and actions.

Portobello Book Blog

Set in Glasgow this is pure Scottish gold. The descriptions of the area sound very authentic to the point I think I could do a tour of the City and Campsies just from my knowledge from the book. Then the characters have that natural interaction that just brings them to life with a raw quick-witted humour.

Books from Dusk Till Dawn

READER REVIEWS OF DARK OF NIGHT

"Fast paced Tartan Noir at its best."

"With twists and turns that will keep your head spinning and a touch of comedy that brings her characters to life, this is one you won't want to put down."

"Seriously invested in the characters and very much enjoying the Glesga banter and humour."

"I read this book in just a few hours and OMG the cliff hanger!"

"Truly loved it!"

"Absolutely love the book, captivating, full of suspense and really funny in bits too."

"Pure gave me the chills."

"I rarely read fiction books but sweet mother this was epic... read it in one go and have been checking daily for Episode 2... I can't believe we are being held on that cliffhanger."

"Twists and turns, characters you fall in love with.....and hate! A great read."

"Watch out Brookmyre and MacBride - there's a new author in town who's adding their own splash of colour to Tartan Noir. CS Duffy nails it with a funny, engrossing and disturbing tale of love, murder and more in a uniquely Scottish way - I can't wait for the next book."

Published in 2018 by CSD

Copyright © C S Duffy 2018

C S Duffy has asserted her right to be identified as the
author of this Work in accordance with the Copyright,
Designs and Patents Act 1988

ISBN: 9781999625603

All rights reserved. No part of this publication may be
reproduced, stored in a retrieval system, or transmitted
in any form or by any means, electronic, mechanical,
photocopying, recording or otherwise, without the prior
permission of the copyright owner.

All characters and events in this publication, other than
those clearly in the public domain, are fictitious and any
resemblance to real persons, living or dead,
is purely coincidental.

A CIP catalogue copy of this book can be found
in the British Library.

Published with the help of Indie Authors World

IndieAuthors
World

*To Mum and Dad who just
wanted me to get a real job.*

CHAPTER 1

Wednesday 5 March

The bus wouldn't go any faster, no matter how fiercely Ruari begged it to under his breath. He sat on the front seat of the top deck, staring urgently out through the rivulets of rain that crisscrossed the window on the miserable Glasgow night, pressing his foot on an imaginary gas pedal. But the bus swung leisurely into a stop as though it had all the time in the world.

Outside, the drizzle glowed orange under the street lamps lighting Dumbarton Road. Scores of fuzzy red brake lights, distorted by the rain, blazed two by two far into the distance.

The bus pulled out about a metre and juddered to a stop behind a white van. *Come on, come on, come on.* A flurry of furious horns sounded up ahead. Some numpty had tried to cross the road between cars, causing somebody to miss the green light and all hell to break loose. Below on the road he could see hoods and brollies scurrying along the pavement. Folk trudging home from work, popping to the corner shop for a pint of milk, staggering home from a cheeky mid-week session.

The bus inched forward another metre or two then a woman dashed into the road, thudded at the door, shrieked at the driver to *'gonnae let me on or ah'm gonnae be late for my night shift an' ah cannae lose this job or the social will be raging'.* Ruari heard the hiss and thud of the doors opening and the driver genially telling her to *'mon then,* and he silently seethed.

The lights shifted to green. Traffic surged forward, then stopped again. The bus jerked on about a footstep and Ruari leaned forward, put his head in his hands, tapping his foot agitatedly.

A wee old lady sitting next to him, a clear plastic hood tied tightly over a steel-grey perm that looked as though it could withstand nuclear warfare, watched him dubiously.

'You okay, son?' she asked in a low voice that betrayed a lifelong 60-a-day habit.

'Aye, fine,' he said, trying to shake off the notion that the bus would go even slower if he wasn't willing it forward.

'You gonnae be sick?'

He shook his head, though in truth the answer was 'Maybe'.

'Gonnae tell me if you are, I cannae staun' the sight o' it. Gies me the boak.'

He promised he would give her fair notice of any impending vomit as the bus finally lurched through the traffic lights and trundled towards Victoria Park. Now that it was actually moving he felt a surge of panic and wished it would slow down. He didn't know what he was going to say yet.

Maybe he should have brought flowers. There was that wee garage next to Granny Gibbs, maybe they'd have some. Nah. Lorna would laugh in his face if he rocked up with a bunch of weedy garage daffodils to declare undying love.

There was a pretty good chance she was going to laugh in his face in any case.

He wasn't exactly the Milk Tray Man, he reflected ruefully. Stuck in traffic on a bus that stank vaguely of piss, wiping clammy hands on his jeans under the watchful gaze of an old lady who kept sternly reminding him she'd belt him one if he puked in front of her. These things never happened to James Bond.

Just over six-foot-tall and lanky, with thick, invariably messy dark blonde hair that Lorna insisted was a bit on the gingery side, and blue eyes the colour of cornflowers — or as Lorna said, Smurfs — he wasn't exactly your slick James Bond type in any case. He pulled up his hoodie and slumped down in the seat, feeling rejected already.

Maybe the whole thing was a mistake.

It was a mistake, he decided forcefully. He should just get off at the next stop, trudge home, and forget the whole thing. It wasn't as though anybody even knew he'd got this far. Except for the old lady next to him, but she thought he was a junkie.

It was Lorna herself who told him that no good came of friends confessing feelings to friends. They'd gone for a pint at the Lismore pub after one of their Crossfit sessions. He'd signed up for a mad bootcamp thing in a fit of January keenness, and he and Lorna had instantly bonded over being the only two who thought that doing burpees until you puke was an absurd notion. Or doing burpees at all, for that matter. They were quickly established as the naughty ones, sniggering at the back and doing impressions of their instructor roaring that today's PAIN is tomorrow's POWER and sneaking off to the pub while everybody else conscientiously stretched.

'Nobody in the history of the universe has ever gone, "Goodness I've always thought of you as a pal but now you've brought it up it occurs to me I'm in love with you too,'" Lorna had insisted, draining her pint.

They'd managed to nab the last table by the fireplace, and Ruari was uncomfortably aware of her leg brushing against his as she gestured to his empty glass and raised her eyebrows in the universal code for 'Another?' He nodded.

Lorna had once told him she wished she had an interesting face, that she'd rather be some striking gargoyle that stopped people in their tracks rather than standard, mildly pretty but nothing to write home about. Ruari thought she was stunning. Dark brown hair that swung about her shoulders, medium height that meant she fitted perfectly into the nook of his shoulder when they hugged, pleasantly curvy figure that meant he knew she'd order her own chips rather than nicking his. Grey-blue eyes that sparkled when she told a story. Ability to make him laugh until his tummy hurt.

When she came back from the bar ripping open a bag of salt and vinegar Golden Wonder with her teeth, Ruari said he didn't think the point of confessing love to a friend was necessarily about them reciprocating. Obviously you hoped they did, but some things just needed to be said.

'Better out than in?' she asked.

'Aye,' he replied, stealing a handful of her crisps as she whacked his hand away. 'Like a fart.'

The bus pulled in at Lorna's stop before he noticed they were there and he had to ding the bell madly and clatter down the stairs yelling for the driver *no' to go* yet. 'Keep yer hair on, son,' the driver grinned as Ruari launched himself from the bus, narrowly missing the huge, muddy puddle at the kerb. 'There's no fire.'

◆◆◆

Serial killer, thought Detective Chief Inspector Cara Boyle, staring at the body of the young woman.

The woman had been placed in a stream that burbled its way over rocks and through fields along the crumbling remains of the Antonine Wall high in the Campsie Fells. Another blast of icy wind whipped up the edges of the crime scene tent and Cara cringed, knowing that precious forensic evidence would be dancing merrily out of reach to be scattered the length and breadth of Dumbartonshire.

Five foot nothing with spiky platinum hair and a habit of dressing like a teenage boy on work experience, Cara knew that she was infamous throughout the force, and often joked that she'd never retire until she was at least legendary. She was known, in equal parts, for having all but single-handedly blown apart a trafficking ring after posing as a Polish teenager back when she was a fresh-faced recruit years ago, and for her breathtakingly gorgeous twenty-something Swedish husband Stellan. *Do you think she bought him?* Cara overheard a couple of younger DIs whispering in the loos at the last Christmas drinks. In bed that night she and Stellan kept waking themselves up giggling all over again at the thought of Cara ordering herself a Viking sex god off the internet. In truth they'd ended up snogging at a Full Moon Party in Thailand when he was 19 and she 33, and though she'd sworn off him several times, somehow five years later they had ended up married and ridiculously happy.

Powerful lights had been set up around the edges of the scene, bathing it in an otherworldly silvery glow that made the darkness beyond even deeper. Stepping away from the body for a moment to collect her thoughts, Cara surveyed the hive of activity with a practiced eye. The perimeter was guarded by a couple of young uniformed constables, their terrified expressions and shaving rashes making Cara want to give them a reassuring cuddle. The crime scene team, under the experienced guidance of medical examiner Alison Crawford, moved as though in a choreographed dance.

Dance. That was what had been tugging at the edge of her brain ever since she first saw the young woman's body. Cara pushed her way back into the tent where Alison was quietly conferring with one of her younger assistants.

At first glance, it had looked as though the woman had been indifferently tossed in the burn, her arms and legs splayed on either side, but now Cara realised that she had been carefully posed. She was lying on her side, her left leg pointed behind her, right arm gracefully stretching overhead. Both toes were pointed, the fingers of each hand forming an elegant arc. Her face, though her neck and jaw were mottled with bruises from the strangulation, was set in a half smile, as though she were smirking at the flurry of activity all around her.

'She's dancing,' Cara muttered.

Alison nodded. Alison must have been nearing retirement age, her mop of grey curls was pulled back into a messy bun, and Cara had never known her to wear a scrap of makeup. She looked as though she should be knitting for grandkids and going along to the community centre for bingo with her pals, instead of out here in the middle of nowhere on a freezing night, taking the temperature of a corpse.

'My eldest daughter did ballet for a while in her teens,' Alison said. 'I think that's called an arabesque.'

'Creepy,' muttered Detective Constable Ricky Dawson in his deep Yorkshire brogue, handing Cara a fresh cup of tea she couldn't remember whether or not she'd asked for.

Either way she was grateful for its warmth. Ricky had been recently transferred from Leeds when his wife had got a job at Queen Elizabeth University Hospital. Tall and fair, with a shaved head and the tip of what looked like a substantial and intricate tattoo poking out the top of his shirt collar, Ricky's happy-go-lucky manner belied a sharp mind and Cara had her eye on him for imminent promotion.

It *was* creepy, Cara thought. It was theatrical. The pose, the smile, the way the woman had been left to glisten in the moonlight with the stream trickling around her. He had even trailed out her hair behind her, as though she were dancing into the wind. It all spoke to a level of thought and planning that was chilling.

'Less than an hour, I reckon.' Alison got to her feet with a wince as her knees protested. 'She's still fairly warm given the temperature of of the water.'

Cara stared in surprise. 'How was she found so quickly out here? We must be miles from the nearest road.'

'Crowd of teenage halfwits,' said Ricky. 'They came up here to do mushrooms, if you can believe it.'

'Mushrooms?' laughed Alison. 'What happened to eccies? Are they time travellers fae 1965?'

'I did a brilliant mushroom shake in Thailand years ago,' said Cara, chuckling at Ricky's horrified expression. 'Thought I was fighting ninjas. Stellan followed me about for hours, only just stopped me from breaking my foot kickboxing a lamppost.'

'Aww, no wonder you decided he was a keeper.'

'At that point I barely knew he was a person.'

Ricky cleared his throat, apparently struggling to keep his disapproval from showing. 'Apparently one of them had already taken his share by the time they stumbled across the body and is still convinced he saw her floating after him. They're being held in a couple of our vans down in the car park near Lennoxtown. Don't reckon they'll be heading out here for a session again in a hurry.'

'That's one way to scare kids off drugs,' said Alison. She finished packing up her kit and yawned deeply. 'Whatever works, I suppose.'

'Have we got statements from them?' asked Cara.

'Waiting on their parents. One of them already said they passed someone on the path on the way up, and they're all having kittens over having been so near a killer. It were pitch dark though, I wouldn't count on getting much in the way of descriptions from them.'

'Could be useful for establishing timings, at least. Thanks, Ricky — could you head down there and keep an eye on them until the parents arrive? I'd rather one of us directly heard anything they blurt out before they're officially interviewed.'

Ricky nodded and took off. Cara and Alison stepped beyond the perimeter and handed their overalls, shoe coverings and gloves to one of Alison's assistants.

'It's not a first kill,' said Alison. Cara could barely see her face in the darkness, but her tone was grave. 'I won't be saying this officially until tomorrow of course, but I don't think we're going to find a scrap of forensic evidence on her. She's been washed thoroughly, and I suspect placed in water deliberately to take care of anything he missed. He knows what he's doing, Cara.'

Cara nodded. It had been her first thought when she laid eyes on the body. She shuddered.

Cara had dealt with plenty of gruesome murders in her time - the majority gang related - but there was something about that white whale of criminals that sent chills down her spine. *Serial killer.* Those monsters who kill for the pleasure of it, who lurk in the shadows preying on the innocent, whose thirst for blood would never be sated. They terrified Cara to the depths of her soul. The idea that a serial killer could be on the loose in Glasgow made her want to race round the city screaming to everyone to run home and lock their doors. She started to make her way back down the treacherously steep path, aware she was frowning to herself in the darkness. She was fighting an urge to gather up her nieces and nephews and stick them in a cell in the bowels of the police station behind ten centimetres of impenetrable steel until the coast was clear.

'Ma'am?' a young female constable, her long blonde plait dancing in the wind, came scrabbling down behind her. 'We've just found the victim's handbag under some rocks. There's ID in her purse.'

◆◆◆

Later, Ruari wasn't sure whether he consciously registered the blue lights flashing in the darkness outside Lorna's flat. He was still rehearsing his *now don't laugh, but…* speech in his head as he bounded up the stairs of her tenement building two at a time. The front door had been on the latch, but it often was. Being so close to the university there were loads of student flatshares in the building, and the whippersnappers, as they called them, weren't the most conscientious about security.

'No thief'd be daft enough to break in here anyway,' Lorna had shrugged the last time they found the front door wide open. 'Naeb'dy that stays here has got anything worth the bother taking.'

Ruari sternly reminded her that bampots off their heads could smash her door down just to take her toothbrush, and she laughed and told him he was getting cynical. He shut the door firmly anyway.

It wasn't until he saw Kevin McGregor guarding Lorna's front door that he finally noticed the flurry of activity filling the hallway and stairwell. Police radios crackled static, uniforms and detectives congregated on the ground floor, talking in low voices. How did he not see that? He must have run right past them.

He knew Kevin, vaguely. They'd been through training at the same time. They'd sat next to each other in their spanking new uniforms on induction day, weather-beaten officers looking over their fresh faced eagerness with thinly veiled cynicism. Unlike Ruari, however, Kevin had stood the test of time, and now held up a hand to stop him before recognition flickered in his eyes.

'Ruari MacCallan?' he asked in surprise. 'How're you dain', man? What are ye dain' here, you're no' oot o' uniform already are ye?'

Ruari shook his head, trying to peer over Kevin's shoulder into Lorna's flat. She must have been broken in to, he thought. Somebody thought she had something worth taking after all. He'd wind her up about that when he saw her.

It couldn't have been very long ago. The scene had an air of freshness, of nobody quite knowing what was going on yet. It could have been happening while he was sitting on the bus, he realised with dismay. He should have leapt off the bus and sprinted here ages ago. He might have made it on time to help.

Did Lorna come home to find her place ransacked? She'd not been home when it happened, he thought frantically. It wasn't bampots off their heads after her toothbrush, was it?

One of Ruari's first call outs had been to an estate on the south side where a woman had been stabbed while walking home from getting an ice lolly from the garage. She was fine, the knife had missed everything vital and she was quite the thing about it. She sat chatting with the paramedics and sucking on her lolly while the headcase who'd done it cheerfully explained to Ruari that he had been certain, at the time, that the woman was a demon. *Ah see noo ah wis wrang*, he admitted solemnly with a rueful shrug, before making Ruari read the statement back three times to make sure he'd got the description of the demon right.

A cold, heavy feeling settled in Ruari's stomach.

'I'm not working,' he said. Kevin could catch up on the whole pathetic saga some other time. 'Lorna's a pal of mine. Where is she? Is she at the station?'

The look in Kevin's eye sent an icy wave of horror washing over him, and Ruari was already shaking his head when he saw her. Detective Chief Inspector Cara Boyle was coming up the stairs. He could just spot her platinum hair as she approached, conferring with somebody Ruari didn't recognise.

Everyone knew DCI Boyle. She was the hotshot of the Specialist Crimes Division, the youngest woman ever to head up her own Major Investigation Unit.

DCI Boyle wouldn't be here for a break-in.

DCI Boyle would only be here for a murder.

Blood roared in Ruari's ears and somewhere far in the distance he heard Kevin shout, as his knees gave way and he tumbled down the stone steps.

◆◆◆

Fifteen minutes later, Ruari was asked if he was going to puke, for the second time that evening.

He shook his head even as it pounded in protest and put on his best 'I'm not concussed' face. The freckled paramedic, young with fair spiky hair who looked disconcertingly as though he should be sent to bed with no dessert, shone a light in his eyes.

'I didn't faint,' Ruari insisted for the sixtieth time. 'I just tripped on the stairs.' The paramedic nodded and told him to squeeze his hand.

Ruari pressed the ice pack into his throbbing jaw and felt a trickle of blood run from somewhere on his temple along his hairline and behind his ear.

DCI Boyle stood a little way away as he perched on the back step of the ambulance trying in vain to stop his head spinning. She was with one of her DIs, a woman Ruari vaguely recalled challenging him to a shots competition at the Christmas party a couple of months ago. He'd been about to leave, but the woman was so gorgeous he was taken aback at her singling him out and heard himself agreeing. He managed one more round of something noxious and blue, then walked into a wall.

Samira, he thought her name was.

Samira and her boss were waiting for the paramedics to clear him before they came over to talk. *None of this is happening*, he thought furiously.

His *now don't laugh but...* speech was still rattling around his head.

Any minute now Lorna would come barreling up, laugh her head off and call him a fanny for sitting there with an ice pack on his head and blood dripping over his face. Everything would start to make sense again.

A torrent of pins and needles roared through him and for a horrible moment he thought he would make a liar of himself and puke after all. At least that wee old lady was far away on the bus by now. The paramedic rubbed his back and Kevin pressed a paper cup of strong tea into his hands.

'Has she been formally identified?' Ruari croaked, the delusional note of hope sounding pathetic in his own ears. 'Lorna.'

He had to keep saying her name. If he kept saying her name, then she wasn't gone.

Kevin nodded, catching Boyle's eye with a brief nod Ruari only just caught out of the corner of his eye. He was on the other side of it now. How to Treat Recently Bereaved Witnesses. He was struck by the absurd notion that if he hadn't been sacked then somehow he would be standing where Kevin was now, and it would be somebody else's best friend's flat being ransacked for evidence. He shuddered, an abyss of horror lapping at his toes.

'Her parents are there now. Sister's on her way up fae London.'

'Greer,' muttered Ruari pointlessly.

'When was the last time you saw Lorna, Ruari?' asked Cara gently and Ruari blinked at her. He hadn't noticed her approaching.

'Monday,' he said, his voice sounding thin and faraway in his own ears. 'Our Crossfit —'

No.

That wasn't the last time he saw her.

The memory struck him like kick in the ribs and he folded over, gasping for breath as though he'd been physically winded.

Tuesday night.

Last night.

She'd come in to the restaurant where he worked in Finnieston, all cosy with some slimy chancer. Ruari had been seething. He snapped that he was busy when she came up to the bar to talk to him, cutting off any potential requests to evaluate the new man. He'd wondered what she was playing at, flaunting it in front of him like that. At his work, for goodness sake, where she knew fine he couldn't escape.

Then on the way home he remembered that she wasn't flaunting it. She had no idea how he felt about her. Because he'd never told her.

'Can you remember anything about the man she was with?' Cara asked, and Ruari shook his head. He was some slick bastard, that's all he knew. He hadn't been looking at the guy, after all. He'd just been staring at Lorna. Feeling like hell because she looked happy.

That was when he burst into tears.

CHAPTER 2

Thursday 6 March

'I would cover him in lemon curd and take at least an hour to lick it off,' Moira announced cheerfully and Amy cringed. The him in question might be on the other side of the café, but it was so tiny they could still reach out and tweak his nose if they were so inclined, and he hadn't thus far shown any signs of being stone deaf. 'I'd hauv him screaming, so I would,' Moira continued with a lascivious grin that wouldn't have been out of place on seventies Saturday evening TV, 'For help.'

Moira was a retired groupie who set up the wee café just off Dumbarton Road after being paid off handsomely by the manager of a chart-topping band, having broken her wrist playing some mad sex game that Amy thought sounded like an extremely creative take on musical bumps. Moira would admit to staring down the barrel of fifty but refused to say from which direction. Her startlingly blonde hair, brittle from years of peroxide, was invariably piled on her head in a fashion that evoked more bird's nest than beehive and her eyes were all but lost under layers of kohl that Amy suspected had been there for decades too.

'Lemon curd?' Amy wrinkled her nose, speaking softly in the futile hope that Moira would get the message. 'That sounds horrible.'

In contrast to the vivacious Moira, Amy tended to fade into the background. She was fairly confident that not one of their daily customers could pick her out of a lineup, and that suited her just fine. Her ginger hair was wavy enough to not be shiny but not interesting enough to be properly curly, and her daily style of ancient jeans and tatty jumpers meant that though she was knocking on forty she couldn't pass nearby Glasgow University without being exhorted to run for student council.

'Look at him,' Moira commanded and Amy obediently stole a glance, though she was fairly sure she had his face memorised by that point.

He was handsome, she'd give him that. Almost too handsome. All that straight nose and chiseled jaw nonsense, with just the right amount of designer stubble to keep him from looking too much like an angelic wee boy. He was tall, his long legs folded awkwardly under the rickety table. Dark brown hair that was a bit long and rakish for the conservative suit he wore. It was as though he wanted folk to know that while he might spend his weekdays doing important work that necessitated the suit, his weekends were all about climbing mountains while playing electric guitar or something.

It occurred to Amy that she was itemising him, like a farmer considering a horse at market. Next she'd be examining his teeth and getting him to prance up and down the café so she could check that his gait was sound, she thought with a grin. Not that she was considering him, obviously.

Amy's love life — or indeed, lack thereof — was the one bone of contention in an otherwise harmonious working relationship with Moira. When Moira agreed to hire her a couple of weeks previously, Amy had spun a slightly true story of a traumatic and bitter divorce, and over the days since had expanded it to just wanting to be all independent girl power and hobbies and having the bed to herself. Moira had listened carefully then pronounced that a load of nonsense.

'Well maybe I just need more time before I move on,' Amy protested feebly. 'Bitter and traumatic divorce and all that.'

'Ach Amy doll, they're all bitter and traumatic,' she scoffed. 'I got arrested for two of mine. The only way to get over one man is to get under another.'

Amy laughed and promised that the next appropriate male specimen Moira tried to set her up with would at least be considered, which kept Moira quiet for all of two seconds.

The unashamedly crappy café was the sort of place that fancy folk mourn the extinction of over skinny lattes in the city centre, but it was right there if they bothered to look. If you tried to do jumping jacks in the middle of it you'd probably bash the fingers of both hands on the old fashioned wood panelling that lined the walls ('None 'o yer vintage shite,' Moira would roar, 'Mine is jist old!'). There were three tiny tables shoved at one end to make way for the daily zombie invasion of students from the Uni, and on the wall across from the tables a huge, ancient corkboard had become an unofficial community noticeboard. It was drowning under years' worth of postcards sent to Moira from all over the world, faded notices advertising jazzercise and Judo classes, and a fair smattering of affectionately abusive notes.

The sandwiches were decidedly average, the tea was builders' or nothing and when one lassie in an inexplicable 1940s get-up asked for her milk to be frothed, Moira suggested she drink normal milk then jump up and down. But thanks mostly to Moira's raucous laugh and penchant for describing the willy of every band member whenever a song from the mid-eighties onwards came on the radio, it was forever rammed and the two of them could barely keep up with demand.

'He's aw' clean cut and tidy like a cartoon Prince Charming. Chocolate on him would be diabetes, no' sex.'

Amy nearly choked on her tea laughing. 'What say you to unsweetened whipped cream?' she asked and Moira's thrilled grin at her joining in made her feel a bit guilty. Surely she wasn't that much of a stick-in-the-mud? 'Maybe with a few nibs of dark chocolate for a bitter —'

'A hot chocolate, please.'

They nearly jumped out their skin. Moira later said it had taken a decade off her life and she was on borrowed time as it was. The man had materialised at the counter and stood towering over the pair of them, amusement glinting in his hypnotic brown eyes. He met Amy's gaze evenly.

'With unsweetened whipped cream.'

Oh, he was good.

Somehow, they managed to recover enough between them to construct something vaguely resembling a hot chocolate, which he blatantly didn't want but was enjoying watching them squirm. Moira asked him about the thick binder he'd been engrossed in reading for the past few days, and he explained it was documentation for a case he was involved in prosecuting. He introduced himself as Alec McAvoy.

'Ooh a lawyer,' Moira breathed, jabbing Amy in the ribs. 'Are you one o' they ones wi' the wigs?'

He chuckled and said that he was indeed an advocate who argued in court, and Amy glanced away to hide her shudder. She had seen enough of the inside of a court-room to last a lifetime. When she tuned back into their conversation, Alec was earnestly explaining how this case was complicated by the fact that the defendant was American so had flown their lawyers in from New York, but they weren't licensed to practice in Scotland so —

Moira's eyes had glazed over by then and she later said she preferred men with abs you could grate cheese on and no' much to say for themselves.

'New York,' Moira said. 'That's smashin'. I've never even been tae America.'

Amy started shaking her head before Moira even turned to her. 'Aye me neither,' she muttered. 'Sounds amazing.'

◆◆◆

Ruari felt raw, as though somebody had taken sandpaper to his every cell while he slept. Except that was impossible, because he hadn't slept.

After Ruari had given what he was fairly confident was a garbled and entirely useless statement to the police, Kevin had been dispatched to drive him home. He insisted on seeing Ruari up the stairs to his flat, then finally left him slumped on the almost comically uncomfortable sofa that Ruari had been awarded custody of after his split with his ex, Aoife. The flat was far from home, but it was all he had for the moment.

All but sleep-walking after the bitter breakup last autumn, Ruari had signed a year's lease on the first rental flat he could find. It was a charmless box with peeling paint and water pressure that meant rinsing shampoo from his hair could occupy a whole evening. After nearly six months, the only furniture was the rubbishy sofa Aofie had been thrilled to palm off on him, the cheapest bed he could find at some brand-less shop in a retail park off the

M8, and a rickety coffee table one of his neighbours had been taking to the dump on the day Ruari moved in. His precious collection of books was piled high on the floor against the walls in the tiny living room, his even more precious collection of vintage LPs was still in boxes. One of these days he was going to get around to moving in properly and living like a grown up again, he promised himself. One of these days.

The temperature had dropped dramatically and snow-flakes danced in the air as Ruari made his way from the bus stop in Kirkintilloch towards Lorna's parents' house. Loch Road was steep and covered in a sheet of ice; Ruari nearly went flying more than once before he found the cul-de-sac where Lorna had grown up.

The driveway was jammed with cars and he could see through the living room window that the cosy, semi-detached house was buzzing with friends and relatives. He hesitated at the corner, half hidden behind the well-tended hedge that bordered their corner garden, suddenly feeling as though knocking on the door to pay his respects would be intruding on the family's private grief. What was he playing at? It seemed incredible to Ruari that he'd only known Lorna for a couple of months, but for all he knew she had never given him a thought when they weren't together, never mind mentioned him to her family.

He turned to leave, when the front door flew open and a woman, who for an instant looked so like Lorna it took Ruari's breath away, came barrelling down the front steps towards him.

'Who the fuck are you? What are you doing here?' she roared, and Ruari stepped back, raised his hands in surrender. His foot caught a patch of black ice and skidded out from under him. He collapsed in a heap and the woman ran at him, kicked him in the ribs.

'Are you him? Did you hurt my sister?' Her voice, raw and ragged with grief, broke and Ruari scuttled backwards on his hands and knees, trying to protect himself from the raining blows. 'We've phoned the police. We'll get you. We'll have you fucking *fry*, pal —'

'No — please —' Ruari finally found his voice, grateful for the thick ski jacket he'd got at a second hand stall the Christmas before. 'I'm a friend of hers — of Lorna's. I was her friend — please.'

'What's your name?'

'Ruari. You must be Greer.'

'You're Ruari?'

He nodded, feeling ice seep through the leg of his jeans. She looked him up and down slowly, still breathing from the exertion of kicking lumps out him.

'Come on then. I need a smoke.'

Greer marched down the hill to the wee kids' park at the bottom of the road, Ruari following nervously behind. The park was tucked behind a low-rise block of flats, and Greer told a couple of teenage kids who were on the swings to scram. She sat on one of the swings and pulled a cigarette packet from her cardigan pocket.

'I haven't smoked in years,' she muttered. 'I picked these up at the airport. My mother will kill me if she smells it.'

Her hair was a bit lighter than Lorna's, and was pulled back into a messy bun at the top of her head. She wore a thick, hand-knitted knee-length cardigan over what looked like pyjamas, and her face seemed sunken, as though collapsing under the weight of grief.

'I'm really sorry,' muttered Ruari. 'I never wanted to intrude or anything, I just —' He shrugged helplessly. 'I just wanted to say I was sorry. That I'll miss her. She — she was amazing,' he finished, the inadequateness of the word burning his throat.

'Years and years ago,' blurted Greer, 'Lorna and I went to Glastonbury. We weren't allowed, but Travis were playing so we told our parents we were staying at our pal Kim's and snuck on the train to London. I've never been more terrified in my life, but Lorna thought it was all a scream.

Anyway, on the second night, we were lying in our tent with the door flap open, watching the sun come up, because it was impossible to sleep with all the racket and people pissing at the side of the tent and stuff. There was this story in the papers people had been talking about all weekend, about some British girl that had drowned on holiday in some freak accident with a jet ski or something. All the stories were about what an amazing person she was, how she had an unconditional offer for some fancy uni, she volunteered, everyone loved her. And Lorna said —' Greer's voice broke, she took a deep drag on her cigarette, stared at the ground a moment.

'Lorna said,' Greer continued with a forceful expression. 'That she bet this girl would be horrified at the whole world thinking she was some goody two shoes just because she died tragically young. She made me promise that if anything ever happened to her, I would remind everyone she could be a total pain in the arse.'

Ruari smiled, though a hollow feeling had filled his chest, making it difficult to breathe. A wan sun peeked out from behind the clouds. He leaned against the frame of the swing set as Greer kicked out her feet and let herself swing back and forth.

'She was always late and she couldn't keep a secret to save her life. She never had a penny on her when it was time for her round and she'd bitch about you as soon as look at you. I never had so much as a birthday card off her in years. I bet you didn't either.'

'I've not known her long,' muttered Ruari.

'Oh aye that's right, the CrossFit thingmy?'

Ruari nodded.

'She talked about you a lot.'

Ruari's heart leapt, then twisted painfully.

'I hadn't been home since Christmas,' Greer continued, 'but she came down to see me in London a couple of weeks ago and she never shut up about you. You saw her on this date the other night, didn't you?'

'I never paid him any attention,' Ruari admitted. 'I wish I had now, but —'

'So the police said.' Greer smiled, an odd, tight smile. She ground her cigarette butt into the cracked tarmac. 'You were hardly to know, eh?'

She stood up, yawned deeply. She was so like Lorna that Ruari had to turn away as a hard lump formed in his throat.

'Suppose I'd better get back.'

'Aye. Sorry if — if I gave you a fright outside the house.'

She shrugged, getting up from the swing. 'I've been dying to belt someone or something for the last twelve hours,' she said. 'You did me a favour.'

Ruari didn't move. If he went home now, then that was it. It was all over. There would be nothing to do but get up tomorrow and carry on with life in a world with no Lorna.

'You know she had a thing for you?' Greer's words pierced his thoughts. He turned to stare at her, his heart pounding painfully. 'She said she knew she wasn't your type, but she always hoped yous'd end up a *When Harry Met Sally* kind of thing one of these days. Maybe you don't care, but I just wanted you to know.'

♦♦♦

Cara stretched out her neck and contemplated just how inappropriate it would be to ask one of her sergeants to stick their knee in her back until the tightness that was causing a vice-like pressure around her temples was released. Probably too inappropriate, she decided reluctantly, slipping a couple of Ibuprofen from her pocket and knocking them back with a sip of rancid coffee from the office machine.

She caught the eye of one of the junior officers nearest the door and gestured to her cup. At least it wasn't inappropriate for an officer of her ranking to expect to be provided with a drinkable source of caffeine. Indeed, it was crucial if she was to make it through the rest of this meeting.

'Lorna Stewart was last seen around 24 hours before her death, at Mickey's in Finnieston by a friend of hers, Ruari MacCallan, who works behind the bar there.' Ricky consulted his notes, cleared his throat and continued. 'She wasn't due in work the following day, though her downstairs neighbour reported hearing her move about the flat during the day, and is almost certain he heard her door slam at around 9:30 that evening. He is fairly confident of the time because he had been watching the BBC and was making a cup of tea between programmes when he heard the slam. Nobody saw her actually leave, so we don't yet know whether she was picked up or walked away by herself — but given that her body was found just after 11pm just north of Lennoxtown, it seems likely that she must have been in a car or a taxi. It wouldn't be easy to get to where she was found by public transport at that time of night in much under an hour. Oh — she had been due to visit her parents that evening, but cancelled at the last minute saying something had come up.'

Ricky paused a moment, frowning as he read over his notes as though he'd lost his place. Cara was impressed by the way he seemed completely comfortable to stand in silence as the room waited until he was ready to continue.

Cara had never been the greatest fan of public speaking. On her eleventh birthday, she had been assigned to give an oral presentation to her Primary Six class about Isabella MacDuff, the noblewoman who had crowned Robert Bruce King of Scotland in 1306 then was imprisoned in a cage hanging from Berwick Castle for treason against the English. Cara had got herself into such a state waiting her turn to speak that when she finally stood up in front of the class to speak she burst into tears. Her baffled teacher broke the stunned silence in the classroom by suggesting she go to the bathroom to compose herself.

Years later, she solemnly insisted to her first boyfriend that she had an out of body experience, so acute was the horror of standing in front of the whole class sobbing for no apparent reason. The boyfriend had long, straggly straw coloured hair and artfully ripped jeans and spent their entire relationship in a frankly Victorian level of mourning Kurt Cobain. He theorised that the teacher thought Cara was overcome with grief at the fate of poor Lady MacDuff, which sent them both into the fit of giggles typical of a couple of first year uni students deeply in lust.

After years - decades, in fact, she realised ruefully - of running meetings like this, the thought of speaking in front of everyone no longer filled her with nerves, but all the same she couldn't quite shake her conviction that the goings-on of her mind weren't anyone else's business. Sometimes a theory, the softest whisper of a connection between apparently disparate strands of evidence was so faint, so precious, that Cara feared it would crumble if it was confidently voiced in a brightly lit room plastered with brain maps and crime scene photos and littered with the demolished remains of the box of doughnuts someone brought in for their birthday. Some things needed to be nurtured in the shadows.

'Thanks Ricky. We're still waiting for the medical examiner's report, but Samira, could you fill us in a bit on what we know about Lorna Stewart so far?'

Unlike Cara, DI Samira Shah didn't have any qualms about sharing her progress, thought Cara. She was a born performer who thrived on the energy of a group, who got more excited when she inspired someone else to put two and two together than when she did it herself. She was also spectacularly beautiful, a fact that made Cara struggle not to feel protective of her. Cara had seen Samira's exquisite bone structure, glossy hair that swung around her chin and perpetual bright smile reduce senior officers who should know better to gibbering wrecks, and occasionally she worried that Samira's sharp investigative mind would be overlooked as her career progressed.

'So far we have spoken to her immediate family, and the friend who came to her flat last night, Ruari MacCallan,' she began. 'Lorna Stewart was 29, studying for a postgraduate diploma in journalism at the University of Strathclyde. She worked part-time in a hotel in the city centre as a night receptionist. Both her parents and sister said there was no boyfriend, but to be honest, my impression was that this Ruari hoped to fit the bill.'

'He's the one that saw her on the date the night before,' said Ricky. 'Any chance he got jealous when he saw her with another man?'

'Worth looking into,' said Cara doubtfully, 'but I —'

'DCI Boyle?' a uniformed constable, a middle-aged man with thick bushy eyebrows, knocked on the meeting room door then entered without waiting for a response. 'We've had a hit from the New Scotland Yard database search you requested. Three bodies posed like dancers, five years ago, in London.'

♦♦♦

Amy was in the queue for the automatic till when she spotted Alec McAvoy standing in the vegetable aisle, apparently examining a display of avocados. A bolt of nerves shot through her tummy and her first instinct was to dump her basket and scarper. Then she reminded herself she was a fully grown adult perfectly capable of having a conversation with another fully grown adult.

The queue shuffled forward but the impatient woman behind her had to huff loudly before Amy noticed. She flashed her a quick apology smile, but the woman was lost in her phone, her face tight with tension. Safe behind a pillar, Amy watched Alec's handsome profile frowning in concentration as he read the ingredients on the back of a packet of cheese biscuits.

Amy took a deep breath, ignoring the fact that her basket was about to slip from her clammy fingers. She was fine. He probably hadn't even seen her.

She dumped her basket and ran.

She shoved her way past the guy in the high-vis jacket and the young dad with exhausted eyes shoogling a fractious baby in a sling. The impatient woman tore her eyes away from her phone just to glare at Amy.

'Hey, are you okay?'

She had almost made it to the door when she felt a hand on her arm.

'It's you,' she blurted.

'So they tell me,' Alec replied with a grin.

'Hi. Hello.'

He was wearing one of those long overcoats of soft navy cashmere, beads of rain and sleet were dotted around his shoulders.

'Have you not got a raincoat?'

'Sorry?' he asked with a puzzled grin.

'Your coat. You're not supposed to let cashmere get wet.'

'I've got a wee brush,' Alec said after a brief, confused, pause. 'It came with the coat. As long as I brush it as soon as I get home so the water doesn't get in the fibres, it will be fine.'

'Good,' said Amy. 'That's okay then.'

'Are you okay? You look a wee bit —'

'I'm fine,' she said, too quickly. 'I just — decided to get a takeaway for dinner. It's a bit claustrophobic in here.'

He nodded as though that made a blind bit of sense and Amy tried to ignore the way her heart was thudding as though it might crack a rib.

He grinned suddenly, his teeth white and even and perfect. 'I was wondering how long I'd have to read about those bloody biscuits before you noticed me.'

◆◆◆

'Prawn crackers, my friend. Prawn crackers win every time,' Amy insisted. The sleet had softened into drizzle as they walked down the road companionably side by side and Amy did her best not to leap into the air every time he smiled at her.

'Prawns are fish,' Alec replied. 'You're just having a fish supper in cracker form.'

'They're not fish,' Amy said in horror, 'They're wee creepy crawlies that just happen to live in the water and are only acceptable in cracker form.'

'So a fish supper wins.'

'I wouldn't go that far.'

She gave him a grumpy look and he laughed.

'Is this you?' he asked as she slowed in front of a red sandstone tenement.

She hesitated. 'Aye.'

He looked up. 'I love these old buildings. I stupidly bought a new-build when I moved back to Glasgow, thought the mod-cons would be worth it, but these are just classic.'

'Where did you move back from?'

'London.'

Amy wasn't sure if she imagined the flicker of tension that crossed his face.

'I've only ever been to London as a child,' she said. 'My mum and I did one of those open-top bus tours.'

'Are your ceilings massive?' he asked, looking up at the second floor bay window, the only one that sat in darkness.

Amy nodded. 'Which means if I want to be warm I need to sit up a ladder, but still.'

Alec chuckled. He smiled down at her, and for a mad instant she thought he was thinking about kissing her. 'Well anyway, I'd better get off.'

'Do you —' she blurted, knowing it was a mistake as soon as the words formed. 'I don't know, a drink or something, sometime?'

'Aye, sometime.'

The fraction of a hesitation before 'sometime' made Amy paste on a smile that verged on maniacal. 'Right, yeah, no bother. Night then.'

Without waiting for a response she turned and scuttled up the steps. Shit. Her fingers fumbled for the keys in her bag. She finally grabbed them and promptly dropped them onto the stone step. She crouched down to get them and after a moment she risked a single glance at the street. He was gone.

CHAPTER 3

Friday 7 March

Sleet worked its way under the collar of Ruari's jacket as he ran through Kelvingrove Park. The clouds were low and dark, brooding over the city in a way that matched Ruari's mood as he pounded his way through puddles and mud, icy breath sawing at his throat.

There was a Crossfit class on Thursday night, but he didn't go. He could just hear Lorna's voice in his head shouting at him no' to use her as an excuse when he'd hated it from day one. She was maybe right, but without her, it would be just him sniggering at the burpee crowd on his own and if nothing else he'd look a total tube. Anyway, he needed to get on with job hunting. A few shifts a week in the restaurant didn't go far and his savings were running low. He just needed to work out what he wanted to be when he grew up.

The week before Ruari started school, he and his mum had come home from a day out to find the frosted glass on their front door smashed and the door hanging half open. His mum cut the engine of her bright red Datsun Cherry and told him to wait in the car. Ruari followed her anyway, and slipped his hand into hers as she crept into the front hallway. Glass crunched under his brand new black leather school shoes and their cosy house felt cold and different. Their TV was gone, as was his mum's beloved turntable on which she normally played her favourite ABBA and Spandau Ballet LPs and Ruari danced in circles until he felt sick. They ran next door to phone the police and Ruari would never forget the relief he felt when the police car pulled up and the friendly officers made his mum a cup of tea before reassuring them that everything was under control now. He'd dressed up as a policeman for Hallowe'en every year after that.

Traffic trundled along Argyle Street as Ruari reached the edge of the park and turned towards Partick. A baby gym class poured out of Kelvin Hall, and the air was suddenly filled with shrieking toddlers and yakking parents competing with the din of the traffic. The Kelvin River was swollen and angry, furious whitewater raged under the bridge as he ran over it. His lungs were burning and his legs were starting to tremble, but physical misery meant he couldn't think. Lorna would laugh her head off if she knew that he was finally getting fit because of her.

Ruari was waiting to cross the road at the bottom of Byres Road when he blinked and realised he was looking right at him. The guy who had been with Lorna the night before she died. The last person to see her alive.

It took a few seconds for it to sink in. Ruari had spent so many hours trying to conjure an image of him that for a moment he thought he'd finally succeeded and the man standing on the other side of the road, in front of the Three Judges pub was a mirage. The pedestrian crossing flashed green but Ruari bent to tie his shoelace to stall for time, his mind racing. Should he call the police?

And tell them what? He couldn't even be a hundred percent certain it was him.

The guy crossed the road diagonally and headed along the north side of Dumbarton Road.

A herd of zombie-like students chose that moment to crowd the pavement, and Ruari had to shove his way through them and scarper across the road so as not to lose the guy. The flurry of angry honks that followed him barely registered as he frantically tried to figure out a way to get a good look at his face.

He must have been around the same height as Ruari, six foot give or take. Brown eyes, brown hair, Ruari just caught sight of an angular face with a sharp nose when he glanced around as a fire engine blared by. Though he wasn't exactly classically handsome Ruari could imagine women finding him attractive. Lorna obviously had, he thought, and bile rose in his throat. He was dressed like any smart businessman, in a suit and dark blue raincoat, but there was something a bit too perfect, too polished about his get up. He just needed one of those 1940s hats and he'd look as though he had stepped out of a black and white movie. He'd been right about him being a smarmy bastard, Ruari thought. Who dresses like they're in Casablanca to cut about Partick?

He was nearly out of sight before it occurred to Ruari to take a picture. He remembered from training that eye witness descriptions are notoriously unreliable. A decent defence lawyer can tear a witness identification apart in minutes. A photo wouldn't be hard evidence Ruari had seen him with Lorna that night, but it would give Boyle's team more to go on than him muttering about brown hair and about so high and *know that scene were the plane takes off and he's left alone with his pal?*

He nearly caught up with him in front of the Lismore, and the already familiar stab of pain shot through him as he remembered Lorna whacking his hand away from her crisps. A couple of guys in paint splattered overalls stood outside the pub smoking, and Ruari hesitated next to them, pulled his phone out his pocket and mucked about with it while keeping one eye on the guy. When he was a safer distance away, Ruari walked on, keeping his phone handy just in case.

A few minutes later the guy disappeared into a café.

◆◆◆

Inside, the café was tiny. The walls were covered in that kind of imitation wood panelling that reminded Ruari of his primary school assembly room, and three tiny tables were pushed up against one wall to make room for the hoards of students queuing for takeaways.

The guy had taken a seat at the table closest to the counter. He'd pulled out some kind of big file and was reading intently, his back to Ruari. Ruari caught the eye of one of the woman behind the counter and gestured to the table by the window. She gave him a distracted nod and he sat, pretending to scroll through his phone while he waited for his chance to get a decent picture. He took a couple, but they could have been of the back of anybody's head.

Ruari's heart was thudding as he watched the guy engrossed in his reading, sipping his coffee from a chunky mug. Just a couple of weeks ago that head had been bent towards Lorna's as she leaned in close to tell him something over the rabble of the after work crowd in the restaurant. Did he care? Did he see her face every time he closed his eyes, hear her voice giggling in his ear, smell her coconut-scented shampoo as he lay staring at the ceiling while the hours of darkness ticked interminably by?

The woman from behind the counter materialised next to him and Ruari jumped a mile. She was mid-fifties or so, with wild platinum hair piled high on top of her head and thick black eyeliner around the kind of crinkly eyes that suggested a lifetime of roaring with laughter.

'Y'okay there, doll, what can I get you?' she asked in a throaty voice, and Ruari ordered a cup of tea and a roll and sausage.

'Been out a run, have you?' she asked, eyeing his gear. 'Wouldnae catch me at aw that nonsense. Only time I run is if a bear is chasing me.'

There was a chuckle from the other side of the café and Ruari looked over. The other woman, who was half hidden behind a towering pile of rolls, could have been anywhere from thirty to mid-forties. She was slight, her flaming red hair pulled back in a ponytail, though wild curls escaped all round her face. She wore a raggedy mauve jumper pulled low over her hands like a teenager, and no makeup.

'An' just when's the last time a bear chased you Moira?' she demanded with a soft chuckle.

'1996,' replied Moira promptly. 'I was on tour with a band who shall remain nameless, in Banff in Canada. Went out the back for a fag with the drummer and there was a bloody great bear snuffing about the bins behind the venue. I was backing away quietly when that numpty of a drummer started shrieking like a wean and the bear decided we were a better dinner than whatever was in the bins. We only just made it through the door before he bit my bum aff.'

'Tell the truth, Moira,' laughed the ginger woman, busying herself buttering rolls.

'Ach I went out to blow the drummer. Smoking's terrible for you.'

Ruari laughed with the two women, but the guy, intent on his reading, paid no attention.

'Amy, gonnae put on a sausage for this young man's roll? Square sausage or link?' Moira asked.

'Square, please,' he said.

It was then that Ruari noticed the guy was watching the ginger woman, Amy. He still had his file open, still had his head bent over it, but from Ruari's vantage point he could see him flick his eyes towards her when she wasn't looking. Ruari's skin prickled with horror.

Had he looked at Lorna like that?

◆◆◆

There was a scream burbling somewhere inside Greer. She could hear it in the distance at night when she lay in the darkness with sleep laughably elusive. It was almost like a tickle in her throat that successive coughs didn't quite catch, but she was afraid that if she did let it out she might never stop.

She hadn't cried, not properly. She thrashed and howled like a wild animal when the doddery old partner in her law firm prised the phone from her hands, but her eyes were dry. He tried to insist that he would see her to the airport, that maybe she should get checked for shock first, but she shook him off and got on the tube. All the way home she wondered if anyone would notice how jerky her movements were, how unnaturally wide her eyes, but it was the last Central Line train of the night, people wouldn't have noticed if she was on fire.

She had been annoyed at Lorna. Her mum phoned earlier that evening, when the PAs and paralegals were leaving for the night and those with their eye on partner-ship were settling in for another six hours' work. Lorna had cancelled dinner at mum and dad's, at the last minute, like she always did. All evening, as Greer prepared the trial bundle that needed to be lodged at court first thing the following morning, a vague irritation at Lorna's self-ishness had buzzed at the edge of her consciousness, like an unseen midge. And all the time Lorna was dead.

Dead.

It was surreal. The meaning of the word *dead* kept on sliding off her brain, like jelly being thrown at a wall. Supposedly it meant that she wouldn't ever see Lorna again, she knew that. It meant that Lorna was gone. But obviously she would see Lorna again, Lorna was her sister. It didn't compute.

What about Christmas? Were they expected to sit around the table stuffing themselves, pulling the crackers, wearing the paper crowns, telling the daft jokes and there would just be an empty place where Lorna should be? Where she wouldn't be, ever again? The notion was absurd.

Seriously, stop it she wanted to say to well-meaning neighbours who brought round casseroles and fairy cakes for her mum. *Obviously we'll see Lorna again, she's Lorna, she's one of us, how could she be gone? Stop saying these words that can't possibly mean what you think they do, or I will have to scream.*

That baldy policeman whose name she couldn't remember placed a cup of tea in front of Greer and she blinked at in in surprise. Why did a policeman just bring her a cup of tea? Oh yeah. Because Lorna was dead. The policeman perched in her dad's armchair in front of the window. The electric fire was on and the tiny room felt stuffy and overwarm, but she knew if she put it off her mother would fuss about the policeman catching a draught.

'There's no hurry,' he was saying. There was something kind about him. She liked that he talked a bit like a character in *Coronation Street. You're a good man, I know you'll understand. People keep saying that Lorna is dead, but obviously she isn't. Maybe you could shed some light on the matter?*

'We're working through the list of old school friends you gave me, and everyone from her journalism class. I'm just wondering if there might have been anyone we missed. Any other pals from somewhere else?'

He wasn't going to explain the horrible misunderstanding. He was acting like Lorna was gone too. Greer hated him.

She cleared her throat which was raw and sore for some reason, and shook her head. 'Not really. I mean, Lorna knows loads of people but I don't know anyone else specific. I've been living in London for years so don't really know all the ins and outs of her life anymore. I've told you all the names I could think of.'

She sounded so cold, she realised. So businesslike. Was that how someone whose sister had just died would sound? Shouldn't she be sobbing and wailing and throwing herself into this young officer's arms?

'Okay that's fine,' he said with a kind smile that made Greer flinch. 'Did she mention any names of men she was dating?'

'I don't think she was dating anyone.'

'We found a few profiles for her on Tinder and so on.'

'Then you know more than I do.'

Actually, hadn't Lorna mentioned something about a date the last time she'd caught her on the phone? It was a few weeks ago now. Greer struggled to conjure the conversation from the fog that was her mind. Lorna had made it a funny story, hadn't she thrown a drink in his face or something?

'Aye, okay.'

'Maybe, I'm not sure, I can't remember.' Greer cut herself off as she suddenly heard Lorna's voice in her head laughing about how this total weapon had tried to pick a fight with her from the moment she'd sat down, and the pain was like an ice pick in her brain. She curled over, hugging herself tightly, feeling physically winded by the pain.

'The thing is —' The detective's voice reached some dim and distant corner of her brain. 'I'm sorry to have to tell you this. Are you sure you don't want someone in here with you?'

Greer shook her head, feeling as though her head was bobbing on an invisible thread above her.

'The thing is,' he began again and cleared his throat. *Spit it out, pal*, Greer thought irritably.

'There's a UK-wide database of unsolved crimes that helps us see patterns, to try to connect cases where the same perpetrator could be responsible, and we have connected this investigation to three murders that took place in London several years ago. In those cases, each of the victims met the killer via a dating app called Crowded Room. We haven't been able to find a profile on it for Lorna, but given that she was seen on a date with a man we haven't been able to identify yet — did she ever mention it to you, that you can remember?'

'No,' Greer said. She shook her head, then again, more firmly.

'It's okay, take your time. I know it's hard.'

'No, I remember now. Sorry, she did tell me. She went on a few dates a few weeks ago but I'm sure it was Tinder or another one I'd heard of. Every one of them was rubbish, culminating in one guy with an anger problem, she thew a drink in his face. She deleted them all then, swore off them for life.'

'She could have changed her mind —'

'No, you don't know Lorna. She's the most stubborn person you could ever meet. Once she's dinged something, that's it. I'm sorry, but I'd stake my life on her not being on any apps any more. However she met that guy, it wasn't online.'

◆◆◆

Ruari's tea went cold as his frustration grew. The place was just too small to point his phone at the guy's face without it being obvious. Fury and grief and jealousy churned inside him as he watched Amy laugh at something the guy said. Memories of that night came tumbling back and he had to concentrate to keep his breathing steady. Lorna and the guy had sat at a corner table at the back of the restaurant, oblivious to noisy chatter and glasses clinking, in their own wee world.

It hadn't been some casual getting-to-know-you blether, it had been intense, intimate. That was what had had Ruari's fists clenching and his tummy twisting and every fibre of his being aching to either run over there and belt him, or turn and sprint right out the restaurant and keep going until it didn't hurt any more.

And now, not two weeks later, Ruari was watching him casually flirt with some innocent lassie in a café.

There was some film Ruari had seen once upon a time, where the main character was an alien or a robot or something and believed that everybody was good and kind until the harsh reality of New York City, or wherever it was, set in. Amy put Ruari in mind of it. All afternoon she smiled and laughed and giggled at her own clumsiness, and generally gave the impression of being more suited to skipping through sunlit meadows greeting cows by name than serving up greasy sandwiches to hungover students in Partick. Some chancer who ordered a bacon roll and coffee swore blind that he'd given her a twenty pound note and Amy was half way out the till with seventeen pounds in change before Moira stepped in.

Ruari felt a sense of helpless urgency clutch at him as he watched Amy's eyes light up with laughter at something a customer said.

He had to find out who the guy was and turn that information over to the police. That was all he could do. It would be processed through the proper channels and if he was guilty he would be charged and convicted and jailed. Spending the evening with Lorna the night before she died would warrant him being brought in for questioning, at least. But, Ruari thought, a wave of frustration washing over him, if that guy was as slick as he looked, he would have an answer for everything and he would stroll back out the station within an hour or two.

Right back here to flirt more with Amy, to maybe suggest he take her for a drink at a wee out of the way pub he knew.

Ruari couldn't let that happen. His heart thudded as he watched the guy gather up his papers and put his file back in his briefcase. He was leaving.

Ruari scrabbled for some change to pay his bill. Stepping back out into the drizzle, he noted with surprise it was half dark already. It was late afternoon, and the clouds were brooding low and moody. The little daylight there was left had that unnaturally bright, surprised quality to it that bathed the rain-slicked road in an eerie glow. Ruari stood by a pile of sodden rubbish bags piled against a bus shelter and fiddled with his phone until he saw the guy out of the corner of his eye leaving the café.

He was alone. Ruari waited until he had turned up Crowe Road and then he followed him. Past the shops and the 24 hour McDonalds that made his stomach grumble. Through the wee matchbox estate next to the railway tracks then onto Clarence Drive and up the hill past the station, to where the tenements were grander and front gardens were filled with carefully tended flowers. He strode with purpose, clearly knowing exactly where he was going.

This was his bit, Ruari thought. The guy's collar was turned up and his head was bent down against the icy wind that was slicing through Ruari's thin running gear. He didn't exchange a nod or a smile with a single passerby.

In the heart of Dowanhill, where sandstone mansions sat imperiously behind long gated drives, the guy suddenly disappeared. It was a quiet, leafy road, bordered on either side by high hedges of dark evergreens and wrought iron gates, the rumble of traffic from Great Western Road only just audible over the wind. Behind those gleaming, newly-painted front doors, professors settled down to nights of quiet research wrapped in tartan throws that belonged to their grandmothers, families debated philosophy over dinner, doctors kissed sleeping toddlers on the forehead before slipping into the night to respond to emergencies.

And the guy who might be Lorna's killer disappeared into thin air.

Ruari walked up and down the road, cautiously, half expecting the guy to jump out from behind a post box. But he was definitely alone on the quiet road. The last of the daylight had slipped away and frost glistened on the pavement.

He stopped by the wrought iron gates where he had last seen the guy, but there was no way he could have gone into that house. The gates were peeling and unkempt and a thick, rusty chain wound round and round the opening. The front garden was shrouded in shadows, but Ruari could just make out that it was wild and overgrown and had almost subsumed the derelict mansion it was supposed to guard. The huge house was barely visible, but a streetlight caught one of the corners and bathed a smashed window in a sickly orange glow.

A deep chill wound its way inside Ruari and he started to back away. As he turned to head back down the hill, the full beams of a powerful car suddenly illuminated the road and Ruari saw it. A kid. Wobbling its way across the frosty tarmac as the car bore down on it —

Heart thudding deafeningly in his ears, Ruari yelled to the car to stop, leapt over the bonnet of a parked car and onto the road —

The car's honk reverberated through the still night as the car swerved violently, just missing Ruari, and skidded to a stop centimetres from a post box.

'What are you playing at, pal? I nearly bloody hit you —' The driver slammed the car door and swore as he stepped into a slushy puddle in his suede designer boots. 'If I've got so much as a scrape on my paintwork it's coming out your pocket —'

'No, there was —' Breathing heavily, his heart still pounding, Ruari scanned the shadowy street for the toddler. The street was empty. *No*, he thought, a cold chill washing over him as the driver continued to rage. *Please, not again.*

◆◆◆

After what felt like hours of trying, yanking and pulling with his bruised and bleeding fingers, he finally managed to get the patio door open. The imposing mansion had a pillared entry way, grand turret and long, winding driveway, but you couldn't bloody well open a door. The council high rise he'd grown up in might have been built of vinegar and spit, but at least you could open a door and walk into it. This grand old dump had been built for people who thought they were better than him, but it was still drowning in decades of deep green vines and brambles and rhododendrons.

He had a key, actually, he always imagined telling any nosy neighbour or police officer who saw fit to question his presence, but he'd need an axe to get at the front door so it was easier to jimmy his way in the back.

The house smelt musty and damp and, if anything, was colder inside than out. It was a deep, penetrating cold of neglect that sank right into his bones as he padded softly across the thread-bare carpet which was stained and spotted with dark patches of mould. Somewhere deep in the bowels of the house, something creaked then crashed, but he'd learned not to be startled. It was just the rot having its way with the old dump, nothing to worry about.

With some cash he'd found in the pocket of the coat he was wearing, he'd gone into a corner shop and now had a feast of crisps, three Mars Bars and a bottle of wine to look forward to. He'd feel warm after he'd eaten all that, he promised himself. There was a few drops left of the vodka he'd bought last time too, he remembered. He'd stashed it by the fireplace in what had once been a library.

Tucked away behind the grand reception room, the library had only one external wall and was bordered by floor to ceiling bookshelves, so it was the warmest room on the ground floor. A few years ago, he had wanted to explore upstairs, but his foot fell through the third step up and it hurt, so he decided not to venture any farther. It was a shame: he quite liked the idea of getting up to the turret to look down on folk scurrying past.

He felt anxious, restless in a way that even the warm glow from the cheap wine didn't help. Was it just a few hours ago that a woman, insect-like with spindly legs teetering on towering heels, laughed at him in the city centre? She nearly fell into him as she staggered by clinging onto her friend's arm.

'Gies a smile, pal!' she slurred, holding up her bottle of some brightly coloured alcoholic concoction at him in a mocking toast as he regarded her coldly. 'Might never happen!'

He'd imagined slipping his hands around that scrawny neck, feeling her pulse flutter and flicker as he began to squeeze. She wouldn't be laughing at him then. None of them laughed at him then. Terror would dart into her eyes as she tried to struggle, skinny limbs flailing wildly as he squeezed and squeezed until she was gone. He wouldn't even display her like one of the special ones, he'd thought as she disappeared from sight into the baying crowd. She didn't deserve that. He would just dump her on a pile of rotting rubbish.

A ragtime band busking outside the Buchanan Centre had been getting louder and louder as he approached, giving him a headache. Shower of halfwits pretending they were in the American South on a miserable Glasgow night, he thought.

If it was the American South, he would have access to an arsenal of weapons.

How many people could he have taken out then and there if he had one automatic gun? He had judged the crowd through narrowed eyes. Thirty rounds per second, three seconds to reload. Even factoring in recoil and fatigue he could pump upwards of one thousand bullets into this crowd within the average four and a half minutes it would take police to respond to this area. He imagined the pandemonium of terror, the screams, the gushing blood, the brains splattered high into the sky like jubilant fountains, and his heart began to pound with glee.

Now alone in the dank and dark house, his nostrils filled with damp and mould and rot, all that glee had turned to shit like everything else. He remembered suddenly that one of the walls in the wee scullery off the kitchen was half rotted away. The last time he'd been here he had managed to kick a hole in the crumbling plaster and it had felt good, even if his foot hurt afterwards.

He went to find it again, congratulating himself on being clever enough to remember.

But the hole wasn't empty any more. In the moonlight streaming through the filthy kitchen windows, he saw him. Cheeky Charlie.

A deep cloak of melancholy draped itself over him at the state of poor old Charlie. He was faded and grimy now, the bright, sunny colours he remembered from the time when Charlie was his only friend were long gone. Looking at him now, all pathetic and filthy, it was difficult to imagine the terrible things Charlie forced him to do.

◆◆◆

The front door of the hospital slid open and Jen Fergusson stepped out, feeling a welcome blast of chilly air cool her face. Her shift that night had felt never-ending and for the last interminable hour the warmth of the Accident and Emergency ward had felt claustrophobic. She hadn't been able to shake her foul mood ever since early that morning when she took the blood pressure of a toothless old man who came in with a suspected heart attack. He pinched her bum and with a salacious grin demanded how his blood pressure could be expected to be normal with her boobs in his face.

'My boobs are nowhere near your face,' was the best comeback her already knackered brain could come up with, and she'd been horrified to feel tears prickling behind her eyes. He cackled with laughter and the charge nurse, twice Jen's age and with about a million times her experience, gave her a sympathetic look and told the old yin to behave himself or he'd get a thermometer up the bum just for being a rascal. A two-minute cry in the staff toilets followed by splashing her face with cold water had helped Jen to keep it together for the nine and a half hours that followed.

Now she waited for the bus on Govan Road and wondered if she could really be bothered meeting her wee brother's new girlfriend that night. She had already warned Sean she'd be a 'Maybe' at the end of a long shift, and sure enough, a night of cuddling on the sofa and catching up on the soaps was calling her. Easy going as usual, Sean had said not to worry, but Jen could already feel an uncomfortable sting of guilt at the thought of cancelling. A bus pulled up, the number swimming before her exhausted eyes before she clocked it was hers and got on, flashing her pass at the driver.

She pulled out her phone, dithering over whether to text her brother that she'd definitely, definitely, meet the new girlfriend next week, and was surprised to see a message notification from the dating app she hadn't opened in weeks. A melancholic sliver of hurt unfurled itself in her tummy. She shoved her phone back in her bag and turned to stare at the darkness of Pollok Park as the bus trundled by.

She was mortified by how disappointed she'd been when Charlie's messages had trailed off. For heaven's sake, when had she become this pathetic? It wasn't even truly ghosting given they hadn't met, and goodness knew she had let other messaging conversations die from time to time for no particular reason. It was just the nature of online dating, nothing to take too seriously. But it had been so rare and precious to get that kind of banter going over messages that his disappearance still stung weeks later.

For days and days they'd texted round the clock, Jen grinning like an idiot after glancing at her phone during shifts whenever she got a moment or waking up at lunchtime after a night shift to a good morning from him. Jen found herself confessing that she wasn't sure she had the stamina to continue in medicine, but after eight years of training had no idea what else she could do. Charlie told her about his recent divorce, admitting he was still shell-shocked by the whole thing in a way that made Jen just want to put her arms around him and make it all better. Which was ridiculous, she told herself sternly, over and over. She didn't know the guy.

They could finally meet and she would discover his photos were from half a decade and a whole head of hair ago. He might pick his nose or be rude to the bar staff. They might just have no chemistry in person, all that witty text banter disintegrating into excruciating small talk as they each wondered how quickly they could down their drink and escape.

But all the same, she couldn't help feeling a tiny ping of joy whenever she saw a notification that he'd messaged.

And then one day it stopped. She'd finished a shift and forced herself to resist so much as glancing at her phone until she was on her way home and could enjoy the message and compose her reply in peace. Finding a seat just as the bus pulled out, she fumbled for her phone in her bag, full of anticipation, only to see — nothing. Well, not nothing. A text from her mum and a handful of Face-book notifications about that weekend's girls' night out. But nothing from Charlie.

Not to worry. Something must have come up. He did have a life, after all. Quashing the daft wee feeling of disappointment, she went home and crashed out fully clothed, then awoke with a ridiculous Christmas morning feeling. But still nothing. Fuzzy with sleep, she opened up their message thread, wondering if she'd remembered wrong, that maybe it was her turn to reply. But no, her last message sat there, taunting her with a blue 'read' tick. Still though, it had just been a few hours. Later that evening, she told herself not to be so daft and texted him, an airy, casual *hey, how's your day been?*

As the hours stretched into days then weeks and it became increasingly clear that she would never hear from him again, Jen told herself it didn't matter. She couldn't possibly take a rejection from someone who had never even laid eyes on her personally. He'd probably been messaging half a dozen women at the same time and just so happened to meet another one of them first. Or maybe he'd lost his phone or fallen off a cliff. Most likely perhaps, the divorce was just a story he span to gullible women and his wife had stumbled across one of her messages and revoked his phone privileges.

Jen tried to get back on the horse. Plenty more fish and all that. She spent an evening half watching her guilty pleasure reality show while burning up her phone right sweeping with abandon, but her heart wasn't in it. She didn't even bother to reply to the handful of messages that then trickled in.

It had been at least three weeks since she'd received any messages, and she toyed with just deleting the app without bothering to read the one that had just been delivered. She'd meant to delete the app already, she just kept forgetting. She got off at her stop in Shawlands and decided she'd pop to the chippie on Kilmarnock Road on her way home, firmly ignoring everything she'd told at least three patients that night about high sodium diets.

As she waited for her fish supper a few minutes later, the smell of frying chips and vinegar making her stomach rumble, she finally decided she'd have a quick peek at the message, roll her eyes at its inevitable cheesiness/

rudeness/pointlessness and then she would delete the app, admit defeat and get a cat. She could rock life as a contented spinster of undecided age, she thought with a determined grin. She'd be one of those wee ladies that made the news on their 110th birthdays putting their longevity down to having never married. 'Men are mair trouble 'an they're worth!' she'd cackle at the STV camera, a generous whisky in one trembling, withered hand and a gigantic slice of gooey chocolate cake in the other.

Jen pulled out her phone and nearly dropped her chips. The message was from Charlie. *What are you doing tonight?*

Bugger right off, Jen thought, shaking her head. If he thought she was going to drop everything and meet him after weeks of radio silence he could think again, she thought firmly as she stepped out into the chilly night. Her phone pinged again.

Go on, I dare you.

He could just get lost. There was no way she was meeting him that night. Absolutely no way.

♦♦♦

Cara clicked her key fob to open her car and shivered as an icy gust of wind made its way inside her coat collar. Stellan had texted earlier to say he was off to some midnight showing of a horror film with his rock climbing buddies, and Cara was looking forward to a hot bath then an hour of flicking aimlessly through comforting rubbish on TV until her eyelids started to droop.

'Can I help you with that?' Cara jumped as Alec McAvoy grabbed her armful of heavy files just before they toppled into the slush covering the car park.

'Thanks Alec, how are you?'

Cara and Samira had once spent an afterwork drink debating whether or not Alec McAvoy was handsome.

He had been installed in one of their meeting rooms for the day, examining the case file for a client who wanted to mount an appeal against his conviction and Cara had noted with amusement the veritable hoards of female officers who had suddenly found reasons to stroll by the glass-walled room. Alec McAvoy hadn't looked up once.

He definitely had something of the dark and flashing about him, Cara conceded, but insisted that at certain angles he looked like a crow. Samira maintained that he was good-looking, but he hadn't always been. She pointed out that there was occasionally the briefest flash of something uncertain in his eyes when he talked to a woman, as though he knew she fancied him yet simultaneously didn't quite believe it.

Cara shook her head to dislodge such unprofessional thoughts as she opened the car door for Alec to dump the musty files on the backseat. He sneezed.

'History homework?' he asked.

'Something like that.'

'You're on this Campsies murder? I caught the tail end of the news last night.'

'I am.'

'Sounds like a bit of a nightmare from what I gathered.'

Cara shrugged, feeling unreasonably defensive. 'They're never quite as clever as they think they are,' she said with a brief smile.

'That's good news,' Alec replied. 'No doubt he'll need a good lawyer before too long.'

Cara frowned in surprise. 'You're defending again? Thought you were right in with Lord Advocate these days.'

Alec shrugged. 'I like to keep on my toes.'

'Then I'll be sure to point him in your direction. 'Night Alec.'

CHAPTER 4

Saturday 8 March

Jen ran. Branches slapped her face, reeds clutched at her ankles but at least the soft bracken meant she didn't make a sound as she sprinted deeper and deeper into the woods. Run. Just run. She didn't know where she was heading, she just knew it was away.

The moment she arrived at the pub she knew that something wasn't right. The bar Charlie had chosen was a shabby wee boozer in the heart of Anniesland, more suitable for bunnet wearing old men to nod off into their pints than a first date. It was a square box that didn't even make a pretence at atmosphere, with nothing on the peeling walls but a ravaged dartboard. A horse race with deafening commentary blared from a large screen at the other side of the bar.

She couldn't deny that he was as handsome as he looked in his photos, even if he wasn't good looking in an obvious way. The angle of his jaw was a bit sharp and his nose a little too narrow, but his eyes were captivating, so brown they looked almost black, and his dark brown hair stood out against his pale skin.

But there was something different about him that she couldn't quite put her finger on. When Charlie went to the bar to get their drinks, Jen wished she could grab her phone and pull up his profile to compare his photos to the real thing. Then she reminded herself she probably didn't look exactly like her pictures either, and told herself to stop being so shallow.

He was nervous, she thought, when he came back with their drinks and took his seat, staring at her just a little too unrelentingly. She shifted under his gaze, feeling like a lab specimen, bringing out all her daftest stories about travelling in Australia and mishaps from uni. He didn't talk much. In total contrast to the deep, articulate confidences they had shared over text, he sat silently most of the time, almost sullenly, as she blethered on.

Finally Jen managed to drain her half of lager, and told him she had an early shift in the morning. His crestfallen face tugged at her heartstrings as he muttered he was sorry to have disappointed her. She heard herself insisting that he absolutely hadn't, she would love to see him again, it's just that she was on call so she couldn't really drink any more anyway.

Jen skidded on a patch of mud and stuffed her fist in her mouth to stop herself from screaming. She froze, half crouched on the boggy forest ground and listened intently. Was he still after her or had he given up? Her mind was clear; it had shifted into emergency mode. When there's no time to worry about the fact that it's someone's child or partner on the stretcher in front of her, when the human body was reduced to parts and functions that she could repair or replace, it was as though emotion was skimmed from her mind like oil from water

And now, every iota of her being was focused on flight, or, if it came to it, fight. She could hurt him, she knew, deep in her bones. If she had to. If he got close enough to grab her, she would jab her fingers in his eyes without a moment's hesitation. One of the tiny claws on the pin prick engagement ring she'd inherited from her Granny had come loose, and now stuck out enough to constantly catch on her clothes and soft furniture. It could blind him.

She had reluctantly agreed to getting something to eat, rationalising that she was hungry anyway, and maybe she'd catch a glimpse of text-Charlie over a burger or something. But when he walked her to his car and insisted he knew somewhere great that was a pain to get to by public transport, alarm bells clanged in her head. And yet she had got in his car anyway. It had felt churlish to refuse at that point.

A twig snapped way too close by and Jen took off again.

She had been training for this year's Tough Mudder for four months. She sprinted evenly, feeling adrenaline zing through her body, driving her legs powerfully on. A gust of terror washed over her, clutched at her throat, but she heard her personal trainer's voice in her head, reminding her to focus on her breathing. Steady rhythm, in and out. Let oxygen give her energy and trust her body to do the rest. *You can do it. You've got it in the tank. Just breathe.*

If she could just keep her fear at bay she would be fine, she told herself fiercely. She had been running through rough, steep terrain for nearly half an hour and she was barely fatigued. She'd never curse the rowing machine again.

The minute Charlie opened the passenger door to let her out she'd flung herself round and kicked it with both heels, slamming the door into him and leaving him sprawled on the muddy car park. He'd scrabbled to his feet in an instant, lunged for her but she leapt out of his way and took off into the thick forest beyond the car park. He gave chase, but she was faster, nimbler; she could hear him stumble and crash behind her in the silence of the night, his breathing ragged and heavy.

They were somewhere near Loch Lomond, on the east side, she thought. She remembered the lights of Bearsden and Milngavie flashing as she tried to force her voice into a firm, steady tone. She demanded he stop mucking about, pull over and let her out.

He'd laughed.

A thin, high, mocking screech that was like nails on a blackboard. Whirling round a roundabout with one hand on the steering wheel, he'd blown her a kiss.

I don't have to do what anyone says.

His voice was high and freakishly childlike; his eyes sparkling with inhuman glee. She had to grit her teeth to stop herself from screaming as a wall of white hot horror slammed her.

People. She needed to find people. If she got herself lost in the depths of the Trossachs National Park at this time of year it would be out of the frying pan into the fire. The jeans and Converse trainers she'd worn to work that morning let her run, but she was hardly dressed for protection from the elements.

Branches snapped, an angry howl sounded behind her — to the left — or was it in front? Jen fiercely swallowed the fear that had burbled up her throat and forced herself to keep running. He was behind her. He had to be behind her. Keep moving forward. She was going to be fine.

Suddenly she burst from the trees into the open and her first instinct was to swerve in terror. Even in the pitch darkness she felt exposed, but then her foot found a small, perfectly round, hole. She realised she was on the golf course at the edge of the village of Balfron and she nearly cried with relief.

She knew where she was.

The instant she felt safe, a great wave of exhaustion nearly took her breath away, and the impact of what had happened hit her. She staggered on a few more steps then fell to her knees just before she reached the first house of the village. She could hear an excited puppy barking from within.

She wasn't even sure she had managed to call for help out loud, but a moment later the lights of the house went on and she heard a friendly man's voice shout to ask if she was okay. Jen dimly realised that she was drenched from head to toe in sweat and mud, her legs and arms scratched and torn from vicious branches and twigs.

'Go and get her inside, quickly,' said a woman. 'I'll phone the police and make her a cheese toasty.'

◆◆◆

It took several hours of dogged Googling before Ruari came across a picture of Alec McAvoy. He had got home and immediately heated up a can of soup. His funny turns generally left him feeling trembly and spacey, as though he'd just got out of bed after a serious dose of the 'flu. This one hadn't been so bad, he reminded himself. At least it had been quick.

It had probably happened because he was tired. That's how it had been before. The night before, he had fallen into a deep stupor the moment his head touched the pillow, then had immediately been assaulted by a series of vague, troubling dreams. In one he had been chasing McAvoy through the Clyde Tunnel. It was dark and there was no traffic, but as they sprinted down the centre of the tarmac he was certain that at any second a car would come speeding through and take them both out.

McAvoy was getting further and further away and the tunnel seemed never-ending. Then finally Ruari gained on him enough to see that it wasn't McAvoy he was chasing. It was Lorna.

He'd lain awake then for hours, feeling groggy and achy and wondering vaguely if he was coming down with something. He watched the reflected headlights of cars outside streak across his ceiling through the slatted blinds, and listened to his upstairs neighbour thudding heavily across the floor. A few moments later, a toilet flushed with such force Ruari half expected water to come gushing through the ceiling. The footsteps thudded back, the bed creaked painfully overhead, then all was silent again.

Ruari yanked his laptop off the floor and opened it up. For weeks he had been scared to read Lorna's blog, terrified of the torrent of grief that would engulf him as her words sparked off the page to greet him. But suddenly he craved something, anything, that would make him feel connected to her, that would bring her back to life for just a few moments. It had only been going a couple of months, but Lorna was thrilled with the response it had been getting so far, and had plans to add a podcast and ultimately turn the project into a full time job when her course ended.

The blog didn't load from the bookmark he had saved, nor when he typed the name into his browser. His wifi seemed to be working fine, and he couldn't imagine why she would have changed the URL since he last read it. The police must have seized it, he thought, shoving the laptop back on the floor. If it contained information sensitive to the investigation, there might be ways of temporarily disabling it from public view.

But still sleep eluded him, and he found himself wondering what could be in her blog that would interest the police. She mostly chatted about politics, her thoughts on Scottish

Independence, the odd passionate rant when some older politician came out with a sexist clanger. She'd had a bit of a thing about unsolved mysteries, he remembered. She had been fascinated by true crime books like *In Cold Blood* and *The Executioner's Song*, and she dreamed of one day tackling something similar about a Scottish crime.

He lay on his back and stared at the ceiling and thought about the last time Lorna had been at the flat. She showed up the flat one night the week before with a Chinese take-away. She'd been in a funny mood and Ruari had been paranoid that she had somehow worked out how he felt about her and was trying to find a way to let him down gently. Until she found the Post-It pad he used to leave himself reminders and had gone into fits of laughter.

'I didn't even know they made these any more, you total antique!' she roared around a mouthful of prawn crack-ers, nearly falling off the couch laughing. Seized by an urge to kiss her, Ruari had got up to clear the plates into the kitchen. The following morning he discovered she had decorated the living room with dozens of notes. *Dobber. Fanny. Wank stain.*

She was a classy bird, he thought with a grin that crum-pled into a sob that took his breath away. He had to sit up, winded by the wall of grief that slammed him. He was still sitting there, back against his headboard, hugging his knees, when his neighbour's alarm buzzed urgently over his head and he knew it was morning.

Now it was well after midnight and he had been search-ing every address on the road where the guy disappeared, then image searching the names of all the occupants listed, for hours. There was a painful crick in his neck and he was light-headed with hunger again. He grabbed some slightly stale bread and cheese from the kitchen and munched it absentmindedly, staring at the professional headshot that filled his laptop screen.

Ruari had spent the best part of the day staring at the guy, memorising his face so he could give DCI Boyle's team as much detail as possible in case he couldn't get the photo. It was him, he was sure of it. Same hair, same eyes, same sharp nose. But somehow the man in the photo looked different, in some tiny, indescribable way. The photo was on website of a law chambers. Alec McAvoy was a hotshot criminal defence lawyer, Ruari read, his heart sinking. Several of McAvoy's recent cases were written up in law journals, and he had been appointed to the Queen's Counsel at some absurdly young age.

A few more clicks revealed that Alec McAvoy lived in the derelict house. Or at least, it belonged to him. It couldn't be as derelict as it appeared, Ruari thought. It had been dark, after all, maybe it was just a shadow crisscrossing the window that made it look broken. Or maybe it was a fixer-upper, perhaps he'd just made a couple of rooms at the back habitable while some ambitious young architect prepared to go wild in the main house.

Ruari flopped back on the absurdly lumpy sofa and winced. He yawned, thought about calling it a night before dawn actually broke when a breaking news alert flashed up on his browser.

Woman escapes serial killer.

There was brief video footage of the woman being led into a waiting police car from a house at the edge of the village of Balfron. A glossy reporter failed miserably to hide her excitement as she explained that the woman had been attacked by a man she met on the dating app Crowded Room.

'The victim described her attacker as just over six feet, brown hair and eyes with a sharp, angular face. She said he told her his name was Charlie.'

Six feet. Brown hair and eyes and a sharp face. Ruari clicked to pull up the headshot of Alec McAvoy, stared at it as he replayed in his head the sight of him chatting with Lorna in the restaurant, of disappearing into the derelict house. Six feet. Brown hair and eyes and a sharp face.

◆◆◆

Amy was holding fort in the café by herself. Moira was off at some family do, either a baby shower or a christening, she couldn't remember which. 'I'll show up and there'll either be a baby or a bump,' she shrugged, bustling out the door in a cloud of perfume and a spectacular feathered hat.

Amy was just bringing a pot of tea over to a couple of wee old ladies when she heard the door ding and she knew it was him without looking around.

'He's never been the same since he lost his leg,' one of the wee old ladies was saying as she poured tea for herself and her pal. There was a brilliant hot pink streak shot through her otherwise snowy hair which Amy hoped she'd have the balls to go for if her hair ever went white. 'But,' the pink-streaked old lady continued, reaching for milk. 'I warned him against setting they fires,'

Her pal, with standard grey hair in a perm so tight it was almost militant, nodded gravely and Amy reluctantly tore herself away from eavesdropping to head back to the counter.

'Hello,' she greeted Alec. Her voice was friendly but impersonal, she was quite proud of herself. 'What can I get you?'

'Just a coffee, thanks,' said Alec.

Amy hadn't seen him out of a suit before. His Saturday casual look of well cut jeans and a soft baby blue V neck jumper looked strange on him, as though he were playing dress-up somehow.

'I don't know what the pair o' yous are playing at.' Moira shook her head as the two of them closed up the café the night before. 'I'd have had the whole thing done and dusted by now, and here's you two fluttering round each other like a pair o' bloody butterflies.'

'Good things come to those who wait,' Amy said, tapping the side of her nose, though her words weren't exactly cryptic.

'You'll never bloody come at this rate,' Moira roared back, sloshing the mop back into the bucket, and Amy laughed.

'That's a shame working on a Saturday,' Amy said now, with a shy smile. Alec had another hefty binder tucked under his arm, and he looked tired. Amy wondered if anyone had informed the legal profession about iPads and such, it seemed terribly retro to be carting around a doorstep like that.

'In court on Monday,' Alec replied with a grim smile. 'It's my last chance to nail this bastard.'

'What's he done?' Amy asked. 'Allegedly.'

'Murder.'

A lightning bolt of adrenaline shot through Amy and she met Alec's eyes properly for the first time, feeling hot with nerves. He stared back unflinchingly, and she had a weird sense that if either of them broke eye contact even for an instant something terrible would happen.

'You'd better get him then,' she said.

Alec nodded, then raised an eyebrow with a ghost of a sardonic grin. 'That's my job.'

The spell was broken. He took his coffee with a brief smile, and settled himself at his usual table.

'He sold it at a car boot sale!' the grey haired old lady hooted, and they both went off into peals of laughter. Amy wondered if it was the leg their friend had lost setting fires that he'd sold at a car boot sale, or if she had missed a few steps of the story.

She busied herself polishing the already gleaming counter, determined to show just how uninterested and unaffected she was by Alec McAvoy's presence. She might as well have done high kicks across the café belting out a song about how little she cared about him.

'See if she takes that malnutrition again, the doctor'll strangle her hisself,' the pink streaked one said at the top of her voice, and Alec didn't even look up.

'He was fair spitting the last time, after he gave her a banana and everything.'

Amy wrenched her thoughts from Alec a moment to wonder how the woman with malnutrition — despite the banana — was related to the guy with one leg, and was deeply disappointed to see that the ladies were gathering their stuff to leave.

'How's he supposed to cook for her when he's only got one leg?' the grey haired one asked indignantly as they shuffled out into the drizzle. So they were in some kind of romantic partnership, Amy thought. At least she got to know that much.

'I think it's time for a sugar hit,' Alec said, and she jumped. He needed to wear a bell round his neck, she thought. There was something disconcertingly stealthy about how he moved.

'Moira made some scones before she left this morning,' she jabbered. 'Or there's Millionaire's Shortbread. It's from yesterday, but it'll be fine. It keeps.'

'Surely a doctor would know that one banana wouldn't turn malnutrition around?' Alec said with a grin. So he had been listening after all.

'That's what I thought,' she said.

'Poor woman's got a one legged husband and here some doctor is shouting at her.'

'Maybe he wanted his banana back. Maybe it was his lunch and she just took it.'

Alec snorted with laughter and Amy's tummy twisted, though with glee or with nerves she couldn't be sure.

'I'll go for a Millionaire's Shortbread,' he said. 'It's the weekend after all.'

'Live on the edge,' she agreed, getting him out a plate.

Amy's smile faded, and a silence hung in the air between them. She dished the shortbread onto the plate with the kind of concentration normally reserved for open heart surgery, achingly conscious of him watching her. Don't say a word, she cautioned herself. Let him speak.

'Men like the chase, Amy,' Amy's mum once said as she closed a romance novel and sighed contentedly. 'It's daft the song and dance you have to go through for their egos, but it's worth it in the end.'

They had been spending the afternoon at the Mitchell Library. They did that a lot in those days, Amy knew that mum couldn't afford to take her swimming or to the shows at Kelvin Hall, but it was nice to get out the flat and Amy liked to pretend that the ornate, venerable library was a castle she had to defend from dragons. Leaving the library, Mum took Amy's hand as they strolled across the bridge over the motorway towards the bus stop on Bath Street and Amy imagined the hundreds of cars trundling beneath her feet, none of the drivers even knowing that a wee girl skipped above their heads.

Mum was wearing her sheepskin coat with the huge fluffy collar that went right up to her chin which Amy loved. Amy had once asked if she would leave it to her in her will and Mum laughed and pointed out she was only 25 and wasn't planning on leaving anything in a will for a long time.

She did, though. It was in one of the boxes Amy kept in storage.

'Nah,' said Amy, poking her toe into a puddle at the pedestrian crossing. 'I'm never gonnae fall in love and all that stuff.'

'Are you no'?'

'Nope. It makes you feel sick. I hate feeling sick.'

'Oh Amy. You do get butterflies in your tummy,' Mum conceded with a soft chuckle. 'But it's a nice feeling, you don't mind it.'

'Nah, it's no for me,' Amy said firmly, 'I think it's all a load of rubbish.'

'You mentioned a drink the other night,' Alec McAvoy blurted and Amy was surprised she didn't shoot three feet into the air. 'What about dinner sometime?'

◆◆◆

Just opening the door to the police station made Ruari's stomach flip, and he had to remind himself that he couldn't get into trouble. He was a witness, a member of the public, a barman with no idea what he wanted to be when he grew up. His heart sank when he saw that the duty sergeant was Kevin McGregor.

'Hey pal, you dain' okay?' Kevin asked, coming out from behind the desk to clap Ruari on the back. The old man snoozing in the corner of the reception area, whose breath was about forty percent proof, startled awake and glared at them both with dark, suspicious eyes. He growled something under his breath then his head dropped back onto his chest with a loud snore.

'Sorry if I —' Kevin began. 'The other night, I mean, I — if I'd known I would have —'

'It's okay.' Ruari cut Kevin's apology off with a brief smile. 'I've got something to add to my statement about Lorna though, is anyone on Boyle's team around?'

'Aye, let me see what I can do.' Kevin gestured to the other officer behind the desk, a stern looking woman with a single, thick eyebrow, and led Ruari through familiar corridors to a small interview room.

'Can I get you a cup of tea, or anything?'

'No, I'm okay.' Ruari sat. The chair wasn't quite an easy chair, but was covered in a sort of padded linoleum that he supposed was meant to make witnesses feel more comfortable.

'What is it you're wantin' to tell them?' Kevin asked. 'Just a general idea, so's I know who best to get. They've divided up different aspects of the investigation, see.'

'Right.' Ruari hesitated a moment, considered asking for a cup of tea after all. 'It's the man I saw Lorna with the night before — before she died,' He saw Kevin's dark eyes spark with curiosity. 'I think I know who he is.'

'That right? You know his name?'

'I think so. Alec McAvoy. He's a big-shot lawyer.'

'So he is.'

'I've seen him again, I'm certain it's him.'

'Aye well, you can tell the team if you want, but it won't do any good.'

'How not?'

Kevin leaned forward, lowered his voice. 'You must know who Alec McAvoy is, Ruari, he's a big deal. He's involved in the city council, advises the government on criminal justice issues, not to mention all sorts of shite for charity.'

'So what?' Ruari snapped. 'He still had a drink with Lorna.'

'Aye, an' he came in yesterday morning to make a statement about it. Said he'd been down the rabbit hole on this big case he's working on and hadn't heard the news.'

'Oh right.' Ruari wasn't sure why he felt as though the wind had been knocked out of his sails. This was good. He was off the hook.

'Aye, he said he'd met her out with a couple of pals the week before, chatted her up then took her for a drink. The next night he was on a web conference when she was killed.'

'He was on a web conference at night time?'

'This big case he's working on, the defendant is a Yank and he's got his family's lawyers in New York or somewhere involved. They demanded a meeting about a plea bargain. It was one o' they online conferences, but because it was a legal matter it was all time stamped and logged for the court record. There's no question he was on the call for the rest of the evening at his office.'

'But nobody actually saw him in person?'

'The night watchman saw him come in at the back of ten and leave at about two in the morning. Listen Ruari, you need to watch yourself. I'll get someone on Boyle's team to come an' talk to you if you want, but if I was you I'd stay out of the investigation, you don't want to muck things up for Lorna.'

'What do you mean, muck things up? You've just said I'm right. Alec McAvoy confirmed it himself.'

'Aye but —' Kevin shut the door over, sat on the coffee table in front of Ruari. 'So it's not new information to them, they already know that it was Alec McAvoy with her that night.'

'So it doesn't do any harm if I tell them too.'

'Look, it's totally up to you pal, I'm no' telling you what to do at all. I'm just saying that McAvoy's a big cheese, and with your — history...'

Kevin trailed off with a shrug, and Ruari's heart sank. He felt claustrophobic, and had to fight the urge to shove Kevin out the way and charge right out of the poky wee room

'You know, then.'

'I was just concerned. I asked around a bit.'

Ten weeks previously, Ruari had nearly caused a several-car pile-up on the M8 when he slammed the brakes of a police car going at 92 miles per hour to avoid hitting an old man who was crossing the road. Except that there was no old man.

'Is it schizophrenia?' Kevin asked. 'My auntie's got that, it's terrible, man. Can you no' get medication for it?'

Ruari shook his head. 'Nope. It's all my fault.' He grinned bitterly, briefly considered a sanitised half-truth version, then decided if Kevin had to know, he might as well know the whole sorry saga. 'After my Standards I did a year of high school in Oregon in the States, where, long story, I ended up doing LSD a couple of times. I spent the next four years basically curled up in a ball at my mum's house seeing spiders coming out the walls and clowns laughing at me. Then it started fading a bit, and after six years of no hallucinations the doctor cleared me last year to start police training. Then I got another one.'

'When you were driving a polis car doon the motorway? That's no' half bad luck.'

'They offered me a desk job when I lost my license, but I might as well be a secretary in the private sector if all I'm going to do is data pushing and filing.' Ruari saw Kevin flinch at the look in his eyes, and he stared at the ground.

Kevin reached out and squeezed his shoulder. 'I'm awful sorry, pal. But there's loads of other jobs you can do without a driver's license. Fuckin' better ones than this shite. Get on tae wan o' they jobs.com sites and forget all this.'

Ruari shrugged. 'Aye. Aye, I'll get right on that.'

◆◆◆

There were fancier classes in the city centre, in actual refurbished dance halls with live orchestras, where folk went all dolled up with red lipstick and victory rolls. This class was in a dingy old community centre that smelt a bit of damp from the nearby Clyde, and everyone just wore whatever they'd worn to work. Trust Lorna, Ruari thought, as Glen Miller gave it laldy through the speakers.

He'd nearly forgotten about Lorna and her dancing. A few weeks ago, she had announced she'd taken a notion to go swing dancing, the kind you see in black and white wartime movies, with lassies being whirled around and flung over their partner's heads. She'd tried to persuade Ruari to come along, but at the time he had been trying to keep a distance from her in the hope that his hopeless crush would wither and die. He'd muttered something about not really being one for flinging lassies over his head, Lorna shot back that was probably why he was single and went along on her own.

One of the papers he'd read online that morning claimed that Lorna's body wasn't just dumped but laid out in a gruesome tableau. The writer swore blind he'd seen some of the crime photos and that she had been posed like a dancer. *Like a ballerina in a wee girl's jewellery box*, the prose intoned, doing its best to tug at the readership's heartstrings before trying to establish the 'Dancing Girl Murder' as an appropriately headline-grabbing moniker.

The prurient horror dripping from the pages turned Ruari's stomach, but he reluctantly wondered if this journalist could be on to something. Lorna had said something about hoping to meet men at the classes who weren't the gormless weirdos she normally got chatted up by. Greer was certain Lorna wasn't one for dating apps, that meant she must have met the man somewhere.

A handful of hipster student types were dancing with old dears who'd presumably learned the steps first time round. There was a trembly old man in a tracksuit who looked as though a strong wind would do him in, clicking his fingers in the middle of the dance floor as some wee lassie spun around him. Laughter and chatter nearly drowned the music out, and folk spent more time shouting to their pals that they couldn't do the steps than trying to do the steps. A group of middle aged women Ruari would have put money on being on a mums' night out howled with laughter about the thirteen left feet they had between them, and a wee guy who appeared to have taken a wrong turn somewhere along the way heckled everyone from the side of the dancefloor, gesturing wildly with his can of beer.

Ruari scanned the crowd looking for anyone who fit the description Jen Fergusson had given to the police, but all he could see was Lorna. She'd be wolf whistling the mums' group, asking one of the old dears for the pleasure of this dance, whirling round that wee guy who looked as though he should be out car-jacking rather than confidently boogying like it was 1943.

Up on the stage, a guy in a zoot suit and bow tie wearing one of those Madonna microphones started to explain the next step, which appeared to involve attempting to head butt your partner with your chin.

There was a shout of laughter from the dance floor, and Ruari looked over to see a student type with blue hair sprawled on the floor, killing herself laughing as her pals tried to help her up. The wee car-jacker guy Ruari had noticed earlier was helping too, evidently he'd been the once dancing with her when she went flying. He couldn't have been more than sixteen, skinny, with an air of the runt of the litter about him. He wore one of those white shell suit tracksuits with a chunky gold chain, though the effect was somewhat ruined by the tattoo of Tweety Bird that he had on his neck.

Lorna would have been fascinated by that tattoo, Ruari thought. She would have asked him about it.

'I like your tattoo.' Ruari said a moment later, when he joined the queue at the non-bar behind the wee guy. 'How come you went Tweety Bird? I like my cartoons, but that's next level.'

'Honest truth, pal?' he replied. 'I've no' got a Scooby how it got there. Had it nearly a year and naebd'y'll grass anybody about who did it. Fuckin' Tweety Bird, man.'

'Could be worse. If somebody did it to you while you were passed out, you're lucky it's no' a willy.'

'Aye that is true,' said the wee guy, nodding seriously. 'Ah've no' seen you here before have I?'

Ruari admitted it was his first time, and the wee guy introduced himself as Taylor. As the queue inched forward, Taylor told Ruari the story of how he'd first started coming with his gran a couple of years back when her memory first started going wonky. She seemed to have snapped back to her teenage self a lot of the time and kept asking when sum'dy would take her to the dancing, so Taylor decided he would. He brought her along every week for months. She wasn't up to much dancing, but she'd sit at the edge of the dance floor, clapping along with the music, happily lost in her own wee world. When she passed away, he couldn't bring himself to stop coming, so he didn't.

They'd got to the front of the queue by then, and Ruari paid for both of their Irn Brus while the lady behind the counter told Taylor she knew fine he had a bottle of vodka in his backpack. He swung himself over the counter and kissed her forehead, informed her she was gorgeous. She told him she was keeping her eye on him, but she was laughing.

'My pal used to come here,' said Ruari as they sat down on a couple of those rickety metal fold out chairs you only ever find in dingy community halls. She's — she's not —'

Ruari wondered if he'd ever be able to say the words without a heavy, sharp lump in forming his throat.

'Lorna?' Taylor asked. He smiled softly, a kindness in his eyes far beyond his years. 'Aye, I knew Lorna, she was a rare bird. Cannae believe what happened to her.'

'Have you ever seen this guy, or somebody who looks a bit like him?' Ruari asked, showing Taylor a picture on his phone of McAvoy. He shook his head. 'Never saw him dancing with Lorna, he never picked her up after or anything?'

'Naw,' Taylor said firmly, looking at the photo. 'He doesn't half fancy himself, eh?'

'Are you sure?

'Don't laugh man, naeb'dy believes me this, but it's true. I've got one o' they photographic memories. It's official, I got a test for it at school an everything. Doesn't make me clever, mind. I got great marks in all my exams because I can just write out anything I've read, but I still work in a warehouse because there aren't awful many jobs were just remembering things sees you through. But see if I've seen a face wance? I'll never forget it.'

'There must be some jobs where you can make use of a memory like that,' said Ruari.

Taylor shrugged, took another gulp of vodka. 'Fuck knows man. I like it in the warehouse, it's good guys I work with.

Ruari dimly noted that Taylor was generously topping up his Irn Bru with the supermarket brand vodka from his backpack.

'What about any other guys? Did you notice her dancing with any one in particular?'

Taylor shook his head firmly. 'Nah, no' Lorna. She got chatted up a couple of times, but she always said she was just there to dance. I walked her to the bus stop a few times, an' I'm quite sure she left alone otherwise.'

It was clear that Taylor was a bit of a self-appointed host of the night, he greeted everyone who arrived by name and tossed good natured insults back and forth with those on the floor. It was a dead end, Ruari thought, a wave of exhaustion sweeping over him.

'There you are,' Taylor said, like a solicitous granny, tipping another generous splash of vodka into Ruari's cup. 'Get that down you, you'll feel a lot better. Know what my uncle thinks? He reckons there's a monster on the loose. Like, no' a person, an actual creature from the dark.'

'A creature?' Ruari repeated uncertainly. The vodka burned the back of his throat.

'They'd never tell us, folk'd go mental, think about it. Lorna never owed money to anyone, she wisnae wi' sum'dy else's man, there was no reason at all to kill her.'

'Sometimes people kill without reason,' said a voice Ruari knew.

Amy grabbed Taylor's vodka and took a generous slurp. Ruari stared at her, for an instant unable to place her out of context. Then he saw her laughing at McAvoy's chat in the café and he shivered.

'Naw they don't,' Taylor insisted. 'Even if it's a stupid reason, there's always a reason. My other uncle got in a fight with the postie and killed him by accident, but it was because he tried to get his dug put down.'

'That's terrible, trying to get a dog put down,' said Amy, taking another swig from the vodka bottle. 'What did the dog ever do to him?'

'She jumped oot a first floor windae and bit his thumb aff. Postie was quite right to complain aboot it, it was a terrible tragedy he got killed an' naeb'dy will talk to that uncle any more. But the point is, my uncle had a reason. He loved that dug. But naeb'dy'd have any reason to kill someone lovely like Lorna.'

'So the obvious conclusion is that it was a monster, aye, right enough. What, like Nessie on her holidays?'

There was a hard edge to Amy's voice. She was teasing Taylor, but there was something about her manner that was at odds with the way she had been with McAvoy the other day. Ruari couldn't put his finger on it, but there was something different about her that made him uncomfortable.

Taylor grabbed his vodka back and gave Amy the finger, insisting that the government would never admit it if it was a monster anyway.

'Well that's me convinced,' Amy deadpanned, as the opening strains of *Little Brown Jug* started up and a couple of people on the dancefloor cheered. 'There's totally monsters set free on the streets of Glasgow.'

'You dancing?' Ruari suddenly blurted to Amy.

'You asking?' she shot back with a raised eyebrow.

He warned her that he was a first timer, she promised to be gentle, then took his hand and led him on to the dance floor.

'If you can picture a baby elephant, on uppers, wearing roller skates, you're maybe a third of the way to imagining how many left feet I have,' he pictured himself telling Lorna, then flinched as a cattle prod of grief zapped him.

Amy laughed after the third time he stood on her, and swore blind she still had plenty of working toes to be getting on with despite his attentions. She was about Lorna's height, he realised as he burled her round the edge of the floor, and her back was surprisingly muscular under his hand. For some reason, he had the impression she was a wee slip of a thing.

'That Moira is quite a character, eh?' he said as she deftly pulled him to one side to avoid crashing into a speaker. 'Sorry. Have you been working for her long?'

'Why were you talking about that murder?' Amy asked, and the look in her eye was disconcerting.

'Lorna was my pal,' he said, and Amy squeezed his hand. 'I'm sorry.'

She stopped dancing, and the couple behind them nearly ran them over.

'I know it's hard,' she said softly.

Ruari had to lean close to hear her over the music and the shouts. 'But you should let the police do their jobs. You won't help, poking around. You should leave well enough alone.'

CHAPTER 5

Sunday 9 March

'With the usual insincere apologies for bringing everyone in on a Sunday,' Cara began with a brief, forced smile. She was still smarting from the argument she had with Stellan that morning. They had been due to go to Islay for the weekend and she had put off cancelling until the last minute. She knew they would make up that night, they always did, but being on the outs with him always gave her an uncomfortable feeling in the pit of her tummy. She would text an apology as soon as this meeting broke up, she promised herself.

'Given that we must work on the assumption that our perpetrator has now struck twice — or a least attempted to — in one week, we can't lose a moment in our efforts to catch him,' she said. 'We will try to make this as brief as possible, I know you all have a lot to be getting on with, but I would like to introduce you all to Jacob Adagbon from the London Metropolitan police who kindly flew up here this morning. He led the investigation into what they termed the 'Dancing Girl Murders' in London, and is going to fill us in on their investigation.'

Jacob was tall and dark-skinned, with close cropped hair and a rangy, lithe physique that made Cara suspect he ran marathons regularly. He opened up the projector, and everyone in the room got a glimpse of his screensaver which appeared to be a photo of a large family reunion, before he opened up the file.

'You've got two now, have you?' he said directly to Cara as though they weren't in a roomful of people. His warm London accent was underlaid with just a touch of Nigeria.

'It certainly looks that way,' she confirmed with a brief nod. 'The scenario we have worked out for Lorna Stewart is more or less exactly what Jen Fergusson experienced, so we're working on the assumption they are related.'

'Jen Fergusson, that's the second victim?'

'It is, though she escaped.'

'She got lucky.'

'Not exactly, he picked badly this time. Jen Fergusson is training for an extreme obstacle event. She kicked the car door into his face then outran him.'

Jacob whistled. 'You don't half make them tough up here.'

There were a couple of muted chuckles around the room and Cara thought she heard someone mutter *an' don't you forget it.*

She smiled grimly. 'Let's hope we do. The rate at which he is attacking is horrifying. I'm not sure we even have a precedent if this is what we think it is. The last killer of this kind I can think of was Peter Manuel, and that was the fifties.'

'Weren't Ian Brady Scotch?' Jacob asked.

'Scottish,' corrected Cara absentmindedly.

'And that guy on death row on the States right now, what was his name?'

'Stuart Henderson. He comes from Glasgow, or nearby I think, but he did all his killing in America, and Ian Brady was in Yorkshire.'

'Any support you need with managing media or public, just ask. I did a couple of years with the FBI in a unit that specialised in serial killers, and I'm happy to help.'

'I appreciate it. If we can cross match and confirm as much as possible that we're looking at the same guy, it will be a helpful start,' said Cara pointedly.

Jacob clicked to bring up a photo of a young woman on the screen, and Cara noticed that he was chewing gum. It bothered her for reasons she couldn't quite articulate, and she was glad he had only come up for the day.

'Well, what we had is three murders,' Jacob began. Cara suspected that he could recite these cases by heart, and she began to soften towards him. 'Though if I'm honest with you, I've always had a suspicion there were more out there that we never discovered. The first that we found was a woman named Kerry Matheson. She worked for a hedge fund in the city. She was a trader, bright, well-liked, ambitious. Her boss told us she was on track to make partner within the next year or two, when she would have been only thirty-three or so.

She was well known to have been dating online, and famous for telling funny stories in the pub about all the weirdos she was meeting. But several friends and colleagues reported that in the last few weeks of her life, she'd been excited about one guy who was a particular charmer. They were texting all night, baring their souls, childhood secrets, that sort of thing. She went to meet him on a Tuesday night at a bar in Putney. She lived quite nearby in Wandsworth, so the location made sense. Her body was found early the following morning in the shallow waters of Penn Ponds in Richmond Park by a jogger.'

'Wouldn't the park have been shut that late at night?' Ricky asked, and Jacob shook his head.

'It's closed to traffic from about 8pm, but the pedestrian gates are open 24 hour except during the deer cull in January and February. But it's a good point, it confirms that they walked to where she was killed, which suggests she went willingly. Coroner judged she'd died around midnight the previous night. She'd been strangled, then dumped in the water afterwards, presumably to ensure there was no DNA to be found on her body.

'The next victim was an Amina Rashid, a deputy head teacher at a private girls' school in Hammersmith. All but the exact same pattern, online dating, excited about a particular guy, found in Richmond Park, in the same pond where Kerry was found though round the other side, near the ballet school. But she was posed with one foot in front of the other so that the feet formed a sort of arrow shape pointing right with her left toes and right ankles the point of the arrow. Her arms both pointed right.

'One of my deputies does one of those ballet pilates classes, and she pointed out that Amina was lying in what they call third position. That was when we looked at the photos of Kelly Matheson again, and realised that she was posed in the second position. Third, Maja Nilsson, an account director at a Soho advertising firm. Same story. Posed in fourth position. Then he stopped. Or, moved on.'

'And this was all five years ago?'

'A little over,' confirmed Jacob.

'So where's he been the past five years?'

'That's the question. Amina Rashid's flatmate thought the guy she'd been excited about was named 'Charlie' but she had no idea of his surname, and when questioned further, she said she wasn't a hundred percent sure of even the first name after all. She said something like: *It was one of those type names, Ben or Tom or Charlie.'*

'Jen Fergusson fits the victim profile of your cases exactly,' said Cara. 'Professional, online dating, her attacker told her his name was Charlie. But Lorna Stewart — she was taking a course in journalism and had aspirations to be a writer, but at the time of her death she was employed as a hotel receptionist. Her current employment was listed on her dating profiles, and there was no mention of her course. Plus there's the fact that her sister swears blind she hadn't used any of the profiles in months, and the lack of activity on her accounts confirms this. She's not a million miles off, she's the right age range and by all accounts she was outgoing and ambitious, but she doesn't fit as perfectly as Jen Fergusson. But of course she was placed in the ballet position, which is why there was a database hit.'

'If he did have a break for over five years,' said Jacob, after a moment's silence. 'Which has been known to happen, there's been a couple of serial killers in the States that went dormant for over a decade at a time, it could be as simple as he was rusty, for want of a better word. This Lorna could have been a warm up while he found the victim he really wanted, or maybe he sees something in the victims that we haven't identified and she does fit that bill.'

Cara leaned back against her desk and wished she'd remembered to refresh her coffee before the meeting started. She looked at the photo of Lorna Stewart tacked to the whiteboard in front of her and shuddered at the thought of her being a 'warm up.'

'He was in touch with Jen while Lorna was still alive,' she said. 'He cut off contact with her, before resuming a couple of weeks later almost directly after Lorna's death.'

'Maybe that's what happened then. Lorna distracted him from Jen.'

Jacob sighed, and Cara thought she picked up a note of impatience in his manner. 'Fact is,' he said, 'as much as there ain't no question that these guys are monsters, serial killers are human like the rest of us. Their patterns are never as perfect or predictable as we'd like them to be. Maybe Lorna just caught his eye.'

'And no DNA traces on any of the victims down there either?'

'Not a one. This guy is a cool customer, he's absolutely scrupulous about that.'

'Makes you wonder if he knows we have his DNA on file, doesn't it?'

'That was our working theory, though it didn't get us anywhere. It's always pissed me off we never caught this guy. These girls had everything to live for, and to think he just disappeared into thin air like some Jack the sodding Ripper. Anything at all you need from us, I am more than willing to provide.'

◆◆◆

Ruari hadn't been sure what to think when Greer had texted him and asked him to get the train to Lenzie to meet her. When he got into her car at the station she turned the engine off, and sat for a moment before turning to him and saying that she was sorry. A cold, hard feeling settled in Ruari's tummy as he realised he knew what she was talking about.

She had woken up suddenly in the middle of the previous night when it hit her that telling Ruari that Lorna had been in love with him could be construed as her suggesting it was his fault that she died.

'It wasn't,' she said firmly.

The rain bounced off the windscreen as they sat in the station car park, watching folk scramble by under hoods and brollies.

'If I had told her how I felt she wouldn't have been on that date that night.'

'If she'd known it was mutual she'd have run a mile,' Greer said, and Ruari's heart sank. 'Don't get me wrong, she was nuts about you, but if there was an actual happy ending on the horizon she would have swerved left and gone flying in the opposite direction.' Greer sighed, her expression troubled. 'I don't know why she was like that. Our parents are together, she didn't have any bad experiences with men when she was younger. She was just wired funny when it came to all that. Pathologically independent, I used to tell her.'

The rain died down as suddenly as it had come, and a wan sun peeked through the clouds. In front of them in the car park, a wee boy with sticky-up white blonde hair wriggled out of his mother's grasp and took a flying leap into a huge brown puddle, grinning in ecstasy as muddy water sloshed over the tops of his wellies.

Greer's wee hatchback was uncomfortably hot, but Ruari didn't think there was room for him to wrestle himself out of his rain jacket without elbowing her in the face.

'One of the papers got an interview with that Jen Fergusson,' Greer said, staring blankly at the wee boy who was now sloshing back and forth through the puddle, shrieking with joy as his beleaguered mother tried to grab him. Greer had left her indicator on from when she pulled in to the kerb; it ticked interminably as drizzle ran down the windscreen.

'She described him, this Charlie, or the man who told her his name was Charlie. She said she got a funny feeling about him when they met, but then he seemed like this lost wee boy she couldn't say no to or she'd break his heart. That's just what Lorna would go for.'

A stab of absurd jealousy shot through Ruari. It must have shown on his face, because Greer smiled kindly. 'Not romantically. She'd want to fix him. She'd think she could counsel him back to normal with unrelenting friendship then set him up with one of her pals. He could well have phoned her late that night to say he was upset about something, and she'd have gone scurrying off to cheer him up.'

Greer put the car into gear. 'It's just what she was like. There was nothing you could have done to stop it.'

◆◆◆

The rain-sodden countryside glistened in the pale sun as they hiked in the Campsie hills. Every second step the mud attempted to suction Ruari to the earth, but Greer marched on at a steady pace, her ponytail swinging. Glasgow loomed ever present as a grey haze on the horizon, yet there was something wild and untouched about the ground they walked over. A vista of green hills tumbled lazily into the distance before them, dotted with sheep munching contentedly in the sunshine, scrubby bushes and ancient, crumbling walls.

They rounded a crest and Ruari spied the ancient slabs - sunk into soft, mossy ground - that were all that remained of this part of the northernmost frontier of the Roman Empire. The Antonine Wall stretched from the Firth River in the east to the Clyde in the west, meandering through the countryside between Edinburgh and Glasgow; it once stood three metres high to protect the Empire from the Caledonian savages. A chill stole down Ruari's back as he realised where they were going.

One of the tabloids had carried an interview with a psychic who claimed that the killer was the reincarnation of an ancient Pict who had laid Lorna's body at the foot of the wall to guard his former lands with her spirit.

'Do you mind?' Greer asked as they approached. The crime scene tent was long gone, but the ground still bore signs of the police's ministrations. A section of the wall had been scraped clean of moss, and the grass and bracken around was trampled and disturbed.

'I want to build a cairn for her,' Greer said. 'This is the last place she was alive, I want to remember her here.'

Ruari couldn't quite find his voice, but he nodded. The ground was dotted with stones and rocks of various shapes and sizes, all rain slicked and icy cold. Ruari's hands were raw and frozen by the time they had stacked enough to resemble a Celtic memorial.

'I've got a stone from the garden of our first childhood home to put on the top,' Greer said. Her voice wavered but her chin stuck out at a determined angle. 'Our parents moved when we were teenagers, but I stopped there on the way to pick you up and I nicked it.' She grinned suddenly. 'I think Lorna would approve.'

Greer put the smooth rockery stone on the top of the pile and smiled, though her eyes were shining with tears. A gust of freezing wind whipped at them. Ruari put his hands under his armpits to try to get some feeling back into his fingers.

'What was she doing out here?' he asked suddenly. 'At eleven o'clock at night it would have been pitch darkness, who could even find their way here?'

'Lorna could.'

Greer came to stand next to him. She pointed to a little copse of trees in a sunken area only just visible through the low lying clouds.

'We built a den down there once upon a time. Our dad brought us up here every Saturday morning in life until we left home so we both know this path blindfolded. Rain or shine, we'd be bundled up and off we went. I think it was to give Mum a long lie on a Saturday, though how we couldn't go swimming or to a trampoline park like normal people I don't know. He'd stop just about here and lean against a wall to have a cigarette, the one cigarette he had all week, and Lorna and I would scamper about this whole area. We had a long running game going for years, about fairies that lived up here and we needed to build them houses.'

She laughed. 'It was almost like a soap opera or something, throughout the week at school we'd think up ideas of what would happen to our fairy kingdom that Saturday, then we'd act it out while Dad filled his lungs with nicotine.

'I think that's why I wanted a smoke the other day,' she said with a soft smile 'The smell reminded me of those Saturday mornings.'

'Still seems funny she took a notion to come up here in the pitch dark with some guy.'

'Aye, but you know Lorna. No telling what she'd suddenly think was a good idea.'

'True enough.'

Ruari shivered, though he wasn't sure if it was from the cold or the sense of ghostly fairies dancing around them. The tip of his nose had gone numb and his teeth were chattering. Something about the sight of the cairn horrified him, but he couldn't tear his eyes away.

A granite-grey cloud brooded overhead. Just a couple of metres away, the wall melted into a soft, white mist. It was as though he and Greer were the only two people left on earth.

'I thought I saw him,' he admitted suddenly, his voice ragged and choked. 'Her killer. I thought I knew who he was and I could tell the police. But I was wrong.'

Greer didn't say anything and a wave of helplessness washed over Ruari.

'We'd better get back to the car,' Greer said, eyeing the cloud with a practiced eye. 'Or else we'll get washed away when that bastard decides to come down.'

Ruari nodded, but didn't move. Despite being frozen to his core, he didn't want to leave Lorna's resting site. He'd never been one for believing in ghosties and goulies, but there was a palpable sense of Lorna in the air, he could almost hear her laughter on the wind. Then he shook himself. He was going daft. It was just being with her sister, talking about her, that was making her seem so present.

'Did Lorna ever tell you about her first ambition in life?' Greer asked, breaking into his thoughts as they started to follow the steep path back towards the car. He shook his head. 'She was about four, and she decided she was going to roll all the way down the Campsies. I think she had a sense of it being just one giant hill that you could roll down and find yourself in our garden in Kirkintilloch.'

Great, heavy drops of rain started to fall, filling the air with loud plops.

'She had drawn up plans for how she was going to hop over streams and sheep droppings whilst horizontal and spinning.'

Ruari laughed and it was a relief, though his cheeks stung with the effort. 'Sounds like her,' he said. He turned back for one last look at the cairn. The rain had started coming down in earnest and the pile of stones was barely visible through the sheet of grey.

But it wasn't alone.

A silent figure stood next to it. Head bent, as though paying its respects to Lorna as they had done. Ruari's heart started to pound as he thought he recognised the profile. It couldn't be.

Please, no, thought Ruari. Two hallucinations in a couple of days. He would have to go back to the doctor's, get signed off work, retreat from the human race again, he thought, and panic scratched at his throat.

'Who the fuck is that?' demanded Greer. Startled by her voice, the figure looked up before he turned and disappeared into the mist in the opposite direction. But in that split second, Ruari saw his face.

It was Alec McAvoy.

◆◆◆

Ruari shoved his way through the usual hoards crowding the pavement outside Moira's café. A wee drunk guy was heckling the bemused queue, and luckily he provided enough distraction for Ruari to slip inside without any of them objecting. His heart sank when he saw two young assistants who he guessed were students helping Moira. Amy wasn't there.

'Moira — where's Amy the night? She no' working?' he shouted over the din. She saw him but just waved as she handed over an armful of pies to a couple of enormous rugby players. 'Moira!'

Ruari leaned right over the counter and grabbed Moira's arm. 'I need to find Amy. Where does she live?'

'I cannae tell you that, son. They'd shut me down if I did that to my staff.'

A fierce urgency coursed through Ruari. As soon as he saw McAvoy up there, he knew. Alibi or not, there was no other reason for him to have been up there, no other way he could have known where the exact spot was. And Amy might be with him right now.

'I think she might be in danger.'

'What are you talking about?'

'I'm not shouting it over everybody here.'

Moira beckoned for him to follow her through to the back. In the dimly lit wee kitchen, she held her phone to her ear, her expression grim. 'She's no' answering.'

'She could be with him. That's why I need to —'

'Is it her ex?'

Ruari hesitated, then nodded. Moira pressed the button to ring Amy again, worry furrowing her brow.

One of the assistants came scurrying into the kitchen, his thick framed glasses steamed up, hair sticking in every which direction in a manner that might have been a deliberately rakish style or might have been general panic. 'More brown sauce?' he panted. Moira pointed to the shelf where industrial sized vats of sauce sat lined up. She pressed the call button again.

'Moira, there's no time. If she's no' answering I need to get to her. Please.'

Moira searched Ruari's face a moment, then yanked a large box file from the shelf, flicked through several cellophane pockets containing invoices and tax forms. She pulled out Amy's employment application form.

'Fine,' she said. 'Here. You didnae get this from me, but if that bad bugger is hanging about her again then data bloody protection can go hang. I should come with you, but they two numpties I hired for the evenings would just get trampled.'

Ruari promised to keep her posted and she let him out the back. The rain had softened to a drizzle as he sprinted up the alleyway between two tenement buildings, then round the corner, nearly colliding with a young dad jogging along with a buggy. Traffic inched by on Dumbarton Road, a flurry of horns sounded in the distance as Ruari threaded his way through stationary cars, tossing the odd apologetic wave here and there. A bus juddered to a stop at the lights. Ruari reached the other pavement and ran on, his heart thudding, the sense that it was already too late pounding through him.

Finally, he reached the quiet side street where Amy lived. There was a wee play park on one side of the road, the swings creaked back and forth in the wind as Ruari ran past. A solitary dog walker, their hood tied snuggly around their chin so only the tip of their nose was exposed to the icy wind, waited patiently for their wobbly old dog to finish its business.

On the other side of the road stood a row of century-old red sandstone tenements, in varying states of shabby and well-loved. Ruari checked the form Moira had given him again with rising panic. Amy lived at number twenty-six. He was passing number two.

A figure emerged from a front door farther up the road and with a sinking heart Ruari caught sight of flaming red hair being whipped up by the wind. He ran faster but she had already crossed to the waiting car. He stumbled on the cracked pavement, gasped as he went over on his ankle, and a sharp jolt of pain shot up his leg.

Up ahead, the street lamp bathed Amy in an orange glow as Alec McAvoy opened the passenger door for her. She glanced round as she got in the car, for an instant locked eyes with Ruari, her face taut and pale. Then McAvoy slammed the door and she was gone. The powerful car roared off into the night as Ruari limped helplessly towards it.

His fingers were clumsy with cold and adrenaline as he fumbled in his pocket for his phone. He dropped it once, it clattered onto the pavement but was mercifully unharmed. He dialled a number he knew off by heart.

◆◆◆

The cold had worked its way into Ruari's bones as he sat on the worn stone step outside Amy's tenement. A handful of her neighbours had come and gone. One offered to let him come in and wait in the relative warmth of the close, and Ruari had only just resisted lecturing him on the security risk such kindness posed. He knew Moira was waiting to hear that all was well but he had no idea yet if the police had got to them in time. There was little point in waiting here, he told himself, pacing agitatedly as his bad ankle stiffened and throbbed. But he couldn't bring himself to leave.

Finally he spied a police car driving slowly up the road. Amy emerged, and called her thanks to the officer driving. Ruari came down the steps to meet her, wincing as his ankle complained.

'It worked,' she said coldly as she came to a stop in front of him. 'The police stopped us. Well done.'

Ruari nodded, hovering awkwardly in front of her. She was unhurt, he noted with relief, but he didn't understand her expression.

'We managed to persuade them it was a disgruntled client of Alec's making a nuisance of themselves,' she added. 'But there was no getting out of going to the nearest police station to fill out a report.'

'Are you okay?' Ruari asked.

Amy laughed bitterly, shook her head. 'You bloody idiot,' she spat. 'You could have ruined everything.'

CHAPTER 6

Monday 10 March

'I need you to stay out my way,' Amy said.

They were at a corner table in a coffee shop, around the corner from Amy's flat, that was open all night - a self-consciously hipstery place with mismatched charity shop furniture and chipped crockery.

Or at least, it was around the corner from the flat that Amy had told McAvoy was where she lived. The flat had, in fact, lain empty for months because of some damp, and Amy had finagled herself a key by offering her services as an occasional cleaner and caretaker to the indifferent letting agency. 'I suspect they're money laundering or something,' she said. 'They don't seem bothered about filling the flat at all, which suits me down to the ground.'

'Amy —'

The girl from behind the counter, long dreadlocks threaded with silver, huge brown eyes thickly lined, came over then. Her bracelets jangled as she handed Amy a soy latte and Ruari his black Americano. A gust of wind knocked over a couple of bikes chained up just outside the window, and Ruari jumped. Amy smiled.

'I'm sorry I bit your head off earlier, I've known you've been on McAvoy's case for weeks and I should have said something earlier.'

The rich coffee was comforting, Ruari felt its warmth seep into him as he tried to get his head around what Amy was saying. 'I'm sorry, what did you say you were?'

'I'm a forensic psychologist, or, a psychologist specialising in criminology. I can't keep up with half the official titles. Basically, I catch bad guys by understanding how their minds work. I took my first degree here in Glasgow just over fifteen years ago, then a graduate degree in forensic and legal psychology in Arlington, Virginia. I completed my PhD in psychological sciences at the University of Texas a few years later.'

'Why the States?'

Amy shrugged, glanced round at the counter as though checking whether or not the dreadlocked girl was listening. Was it his imagination or did something flicker in her eyes? Evasion. Guilt?

'There's a whole world outside Scotland.'

'True enough.'

Amy was sitting almost militarily straight on her rickety chair as she talked. Her expression was simultaneously relaxed and animated; she met Ruari's eye with an assured confidence. He remembered that night at the dancing, when he had thought she seemed like a different person from the Amy he had met in the café. Now she was entirely different again. She was like a chameleon, slipping between different personas and personalities at will.

'It was for my PhD that I initially studied the first set of murders in London nearly six years ago. My dissertation was focussed on exploring the parallels and contrasts between the way a sexual killer identifies and seduces victims, and the way they dispose of the bodies afterwards. Sometimes there is correlation, and other times the act of death alters or twists their craving so there's an apparent contradiction — a sadistic killer who tortures his victims then treats the body with great gentleness and care, for example.

'In the papers they describe the way McAvoy poses his victims as dancers, but if they looked at it from a psychological point of view, they would see that fundamentally he turns them into dolls, or puppets on strings. Women he can control completely. That's why he chooses victims who are challenges. Confident, ambitious, even cynical when it comes to romance. Those are the women that threaten him, so those are the ones he needs to conquer.'

Ruari nodded slowly, trying to take all this in.

'Alec McAvoy was questioned back then in London,' continued Amy. 'He was careless enough to send flowers to the first victim. He had an apparent alibi so he was never a serious suspect, but he fit the profile of the killer so perfectly that I dug a little deeper.'

'He has an alibi for Lorna's murder too.'

'Yes, he is very good at that.'

'But he did kill Lorna?' Ruari's voice wavered on her name, he forced a smile and took a sip of his coffee.

'Yes,' said Amy simply. 'I'm sorry.'

'Are you with the police? Are you undercover or something?'

'No,' she replied. 'At least, not in any official capacity, though I will pass on anything I discover to the police as soon as it is substantial enough for them to take action. I can act with a certain degree of freedom if I stay independent,' she added.

Ruari remembered hearing older officers complain about strict procedures regarding interrogation techniques and chain of evidence. 'Whole bloody system's set up tae protect criminals,' one grumbled when they discovered that CCTV evidence of a mugging they were trying to prosecute wasn't admissible because there hadn't been adequate signs warning that it was operational in the area.

'But if you get a confession without witnesses or reading his rights or anything, it won't be admissible, will it?'

'That's not my main focus, though if I can get him to confide in me he might mention details that can be investigated officially. I'm a private citizen, if I go to them saying someone confessed a murder to me it won't affect its admissibility, it just won't have enough weight without evidence to back it up. I'm trying to find out as much as I can about his activities, how he chooses his victims, how he plans the crimes. I have already caught sight of the second mobile he uses to communicate with them, though I haven't been able to gain access to it yet.'

'Why would he confide in you though? He must know that anybody he confessed to would go right to the police.'

'Killers like Alec McAvoy,' began Amy slowly, and Ruari could see that she was choosing her words carefully. 'They don't want to be caught, but at the same time they hate having to keep it all a secret. They want the world to marvel at how clever they are, how much power they have. I've interviewed dozens of them on death rows all over the States, and time and time again they've told me that the most difficult part is not bragging. You know how there's always that moment in a superhero movie, towards the end when it seems like the baddie has won and chaos has descended — they rise up and laugh maniacally and cackle 'you'll never catch me Superman,' or whatever.'

Ruari took another sip of his coffee, wrapping his hands around the chunky mug for warmth. Amy's eyes sparkled as she spoke. For a horrible moment she reminded him of Lorna and his stomach twisted, unease prickled in his guts.

'Every one of these guys is desperate for that moment. They think they deserve it, they resent that the Criminal Justice System and the moral codes of those of us they see as beneath them rob them of it. That's why so many of them chose to go out in what they see as a blaze of glory in a shower of police bullets, sometimes even if they could have got away with it. I met one guy whose lawyers had managed a plea that would have kept the death penalty off the table, and he nixed it. If he had to be in prison, he wanted to be one of the hard men on death row, not some wimpy common-or-garden murderer. This isn't every killer, obviously, but there is a pattern and Alec McAvoy fits it. I think I can get him to brag to me.'

'It's dangerous.'

'I know.'

'If you're right, what's to stop him killing you?'

'If I'm right he won't. He's not a spree murderer, his victims fall into a very specific category and a specific routine. I can show you case study after case study of killers who were jovial family men, treated their wives like princesses, coached kids' baseball teams, friend to one and all and in their day-to-day lives completely harmless. They compartmentalise the different parts of their lives.

'The Amy Alec McAvoy knows isn't a challenge. She hangs on his every word, half hides behind him in shyness. She scares easily, she is what he believes a woman should be, and that's what will keep her safe.'

'Nobody is that perfectly predictable,' said Ruari. His coffee cup was empty, but still he clutched it in his hands. Rain battered against the window, and he shivered. 'You're like those lion tamers who raise a cub from birth, trust it completely then one day it's hungry and bites their head off.'

'You're right,' she said simply. 'But isn't it worth it for all the future Lornas I can save?'

◆◆◆

The noise of a metal tray rattling against bars reverberated relentlessly around the hallway. In a tiny, cramped office that the guards joked was worse than a cell, Luis, his substantial gut hanging over his waistband, tucked into a leafy salad, one eye on the several CCTV screens that lined the back wall of the office, showing various black and white camera angles of death row.

A monotonous clang reverberated around the corridor. Luis leaned forward, his eyes intently on the middle left square of the screen, where a metal tray could just be sighted moving back and forth across the bars. Any minute now he would start singing, Luis thought. You could set your watch by him.

Casey, a skinny kid just graduated high school, so disturbingly fresh-faced Luis was never sure whether to offer him coffee or juice, swung his chair on two legs, closed his eyes.

'Hey, I tell you I got me a new tattoo?' he said suddenly, opening his eyes again.

Luis grunted in response, his eyes never leaving the screens. Somebody was roaring at the tray-banger to shut up, but the tray didn't so much as skip a beat.

'Wanna see? It's for Bradelyn.' Without waiting for an answer, Casey rolled up his left sleeve, held out his arm to Luis, who glanced over briefly.

'That 'ain't how you spell eternity.'

Casey looked crestfallen. "No, dude. Tell me you're kidding. It ain't?"

Luis chuckled, his glorious, jet black handlebar moustache vibrating. 'You know what?' he wheezed. 'You just made my week. Maybe even month. Thanks, kid.' He chucked the salad container into the trash, took a swig of his water.

'Fuck you. What am I supposed to do now? I'm gonna kill that guy, I swear.'

'White-out, maybe?'

'They don't even sell that any more, who uses paper?' Casey sighed, stared mournfully at his tattoo. 'She's going to kill me.'

'Only if she knows how to spell it right.'

From what Luis had seen of Casey's fiancée, he suspected Casey was safe.

'How's it supposed to be spelled?'

The clanging stopped for a moment, then started up again. Casey got to his feet. 'He needs to shut up.'

'Leave it,' shrugged Luis. 'Governor just announced that was his last appeal, he's got a few weeks to live. Let him make a racket.'

'He's getting the others antsy.'

'So what?'

'*One two three four five, once I caught a fish alive...*'

Almost two minutes late, thought Luis. He's slipping.

◆◆◆

Ruari sat in the stuffy café poring over the latest set of headline articles about the serial killer at large in Glasgow, half listening to Moira banter with a young couple who sat in front of him, at McAvoy's usual table. He was still reeling with everything Amy had told him the night before. When he finally got home, he had lain awake for hours, staring at the cracked ceiling and trying to conjure a clear picture of Amy. She was like a kaleidoscope, shifting and twisting and changing every time he blinked.

Ruari's breath caught in his throat as he glanced down at the tabloid he had opened out in front of him. The centre page spread was covered by a series of smiling photographs of the three London victims, Lorna, and a fifth of Jen Fergusson, with SURVIVED stamped across her face.

'It's jist terrible,' said Moira, reading over his shoulder. She picked up the empty plate from his table, and shook her head. 'Us having one of they headcases on the loose. I mean, have we no' got enough headcases of wir 'ain withoot one comin' up fae London?'

'They think he's from here and was just down there for a few years,' said Ruari.

'That right? Well he can jist get tae fuck.'

'Good thinking, you should work for the police.'

'You can get tae as well with yer cheek.'

Moira bustled back to the kitchen and Ruari wondered what Amy had told her to explain the other night. She hadn't said anything, but there had been a slight unease behind her smile when she greeted him. Amy wasn't working until later, at mid-morning the café was empty save for him and the couple.

Ruari determinedly shut the tabloid, folded it and shoved it onto the chair opposite him. Beneath it was a broadsheet that carried a special on Scottish serial killers, with a tantalising question mark over the Dancing Girl Killer. Ruari grimaced at the sight of the moniker; apparently it had taken off. He skimmed the accounts of the Cannibal of the Borders, the Edinburgh Body Snatchers, Peter Manuel, Ian Brady, Stuart Henderson.

'Christ, we dae a fair roaring trade in murdering heidcases after all,' whistled Moira as she wiped down his table. 'I mind that one's trial.' She jabbed her finger at Stuart Henderson's mugshot. 'What was it, six or seven years ago? I had tae put the news on mute after that lawyer said he turned his victims inside out. Didnae half give me the boak. What would possess a soul tae think that was a good idea?'

'It's supposed to be to do with control,' said Ruari, thinking of Amy's words.

'What kind of control dae ye need that makes you string a lassie's insides up around a forest like bloody Christmas lights?' she demanded. 'I've seen men aff their heids with power, tossing groupies back and forth like a game of pass the parcel. Wee lassies that should have been playing with their dollies instead of being treated like one themselves. I'm under no illusions aboot what human beings can do to one another.'

She stared at him accusingly. Ruari shifted uncomfortably under her scrutiny, feeling unfathomably guilty.

'But that kind of depravity is something else,' she said, shaking her head. 'How does he close his eyes at night knowing what he's done?'

Ruari shrugged. 'I don't really remember much about it.' When Stuart Henderson was on trial for his life, Ruari had been busy hiding under his bed because his mum had green stalks growing from her head when she brought him a jam sandwich - hoping to coax him into the living room at least.

'It was big news here with him being Scottish.' Moira stared at Henderson's photo with distaste. 'If I remember right there's only ever been one other Scottish person on death row in the States and he got freed, so they made a bit of a song and dance about that when that Henderson was sentenced. The death penalty gies me the heebie jeebies but if anybody deserves one of they wee injections, it's him.'

'Did Amy not live in the States?' Ruari asked, and Moira hesitated for an instant then made a face.

'No,' she replied, too quickly. 'She's no' even been, I don't think.'

'Sorry, must have misunderstood something she said.'

Moira nodded, something playing in her eyes Ruari couldn't quite identify.

'Suppose travel wasn't high on her list of priorities when she was married,' he added with deliberate lightness.

'No I suppose not,' she said shortly. 'Are you wanting anything else to eat?'

Ruari asked for a caramel shortbread and another cup of tea.

When Moira brought Ruari's caramel shortbread over, she sat down on the chair opposite him. She folded the tabloid that had been on her chair on her lap, absent-mindedly stroking Lorna's face. Ruari looked away as the familiar ache twisted in his guts.

'Listen son,' she said. 'I know you've a wee thing for Amy and it's no wonder. She's a lovely girl. But you're not the only one that's been asking after her. She deserves a wee bit o' happiness after everything she's been through, so it would be best if you didnae get in the way and complicate things.'

A chill stole over Ruari as he realised that she was talking about Alec McAvoy.

'The guy who was in here the other week,' he asked, forcing a casual smile. 'Bit stuck up, is he not?'

'Alec treats her like a princess and that's what she needs right now. I know it's not the fashion, but we all need a wee bit of looking after sometimes. If you really care for that girl, you'll do the right thing and step aside.'

◆◆◆

'Keep up the pace— five seconds — come on guys, dig deep — three, two —'

The bootcamp instructor, a former champion MMA fighter with a short military buzz cut and intricate tattoos covering most of his body, roared at the exhausted class as Cara levelled one last punch at the pads that Stellan held up.

'And... TIME. Grab some water.'

Cara ripped the stinking boxing gloves from her hands and wiped her sodden fringe off her forehead. Stellan handed her a water bottle for a sip, then squirted it at his own face with a sigh of satisfaction. His thick, dark blond curls were tied back in a messy bun at the nape of his neck, his skin disgustingly perma-tanned despite the fact she had cancelled their last three beach holidays for work. He towered above her, his devotion to yoga evident in his lithe, rangy body.

'Nice job,' he said, and Cara loved how after more than four years in Scotland he still pronounced it *yob*. 'Who were you punching?'

She shrugged with a grin, taking deep breaths to get her heartbeat back under control as they moved on towards the next station. Kick-boxing.

'Didn't we do this one already?' she asked with a grimace. Stellan shook his head, rolled his shoulders out, stretched his right arm above his head and Cara couldn't help the little flutter of lust that shot through her at the glimpse of his flat tummy glistening with sweat. He caught her looking and raised his eyebrow with a glint in his eye, then kissed the top of her head with a chuckle.

'I'll hold the pad for Stellan when he kicks.' The instructor appeared next to them, tried to grab the thick pad from Cara.

'I'll manage,' she grinned.

'I don't want you to get hurt.'

'I won't. Thanks for your concern.'

The instructor rolled his eyes, yelled to the rest of the class there was ten seconds of the break left. 'This isnae a feminist thing,' he said. 'Look at the size of you and look at the size of him.'

'I'm looking,' she said evenly.

'Cara was the top ranked Scottish female Muay Thai boxer two years ago and I am a yogi,' said Stellan, his smile sparkling with innocence. 'Not even a very good one.'

The instructor shrugged. 'Well don't come crying to me if you get shot halfway across the room.'

'I'll try not to,' said Stellan.

The instructor blew his whistle and turned the music up and the air was filled with thuds and grunts but Cara stood still, frowning. Stellan waited patiently.

'He knew how fit Jen Fergusson was when he attacked her. Why did he take such a risk? He hasn't taken a risk like that before.'

'Maybe he thought he would still be stronger because he is a man.' Stellan grinned at the instructor, who was frowning at them from the other side of the mat, clearly struggling to decide whether or not to tell them off for ignoring the whistle.

Cara shook her head. 'I don't think so, he's too sharp. That's how he got away with it in London. Do you know how difficult it is to completely scour a body for micro-scopic specs of DNA? Not to mention just vanish into the night with the amount of CCTV cameras there are around. He's methodical, he leaves nothing to chance. The possi-bility that Jen Fergusson could outrun him was a chance — and one that he lost. There is something —' She sighed in frustration as the whistle blew and it was time to move on to battle ropes. 'Something not right.'

'You'll figure it out,' said Stellan.

'I'd better,' Cara said with a deep sigh.

The whistle blew again and Cara slammed the heavy ropes into the ground with all her might.

◆◆◆

Amy scanned the crowd in the first floor bar at the Blythswood Hotel for Alec McAvoy. Just up the hill from the city's main shopping streets, Blythswood Square was once upon a time the epicentre of the city's red light district, and its history was celebrated in the deep cerises and purples of the opulent hotel's decor.

It was Friday night. The bar was buzzing with statement necklaces, false eyelashes and hipster-chic spectacles. Designer beers clinked with ostentatious cocktails and current hits remixed as big band swing numbers underscored the hum of chatter punctuated by laughter.

Amy peered through the jagged, deep green leaves of the huge palm plant shielding her from view and steeled herself for her first glimpse of McAvoy. She needed to see him coming, to prepare herself, ensure her mask was firmly on before she had to meet his gaze.

It was hot in the crowded bar. Amy could feel a sheen of sweat on her forehead and her flowy peasant dress clung uncomfortably to her back. She was perched at the edge of a velvet sofa designed for sinking into, pretending to sip the glass of Proscecco she had been greeted with at the top of the stairs. Focus on the immediate, and nothing else, she reminded herself, as the glass nearly slipped from her clammy hands and tiny shoots of nerves darted around her tummy.

Amy was still an undergrad when she took on the summer internship as a research assistant to the head of the psychology department at the University of Michigan.

In Ann Arbor in July, the air sizzled with humid heat even long after dark. The warmth of the tarmac seeped through the soles of Amy's thin sandals and sweat trickled down her back under the weight of her heavy book bag, but nothing could drag the swing from her step. She'd spent the day taking notes as her boss, Professor White, a whippet-thin man with an intense energy that practically sparked off him as he worked, analysed brain scans of psychopaths taken from prisoners all over the country.

'The thing is, Amy,' he'd said that afternoon, 'we are not responsible for what we are. We can't control the amount of activity that takes place in our orbital lobe and we can't help whether or not we're missing the gene that helps to break down chemical messengers linked to mood.'

He paused to take a gulp of tar-like coffee and she noticed that the right half of his face was still covered with grey stubble. He must have had a brilliant thought halfway through shaving that morning, she thought in awe. She wondered if one day she would come flying into an oak panelled office with shampoo crusting in her hair as she tripped over her words in her excitement to share a game-changing breakthrough with her own starstruck intern.

'We're far from certain even that these biological traits are linked to anti-social behaviour!'

This he said with a gleeful grin, practically rubbing his hands together at the thought of all that research still to do. 'And none of us can do a damned thing about being born into a shitty childhood. But you know what? For every kid that survives neglect and abuse and goes on to take it out on others, there's twenty more that go on to love and be loved and live their lives without hurting a fly.

'These guys we study will tell you that they can't help it, that they were born with a darkness inside them that controls them, but you know how many of them commit crimes right in front of cops? Almost none. So if they can control this darkness when they know it's a one way ticket to the chair, why not control it other times? Well that's the question. Because they don't want to. They choose not to.'

He raised his mug to take another slurp of coffee, then continued speaking, apparently having forgotten about the coffee halfway to his mouth.

'Some of us are born being able to contentedly sip a single glass of wine all night, while others of us, once we get started, would struggle not to consume every drop of booze in the house before we're done,' he said. 'But the second group are still in control of their choice to get wasted or not, they are still capable of resisting even if it is harder for them. Just as the anti-social personality type makes a choice to hurt. We are all responsible for what we *do*, Amy. You and I are dedicated to understanding what makes a person exhibit anti-social behaviours, but that doesn't mean we're giving them a free ride. We empathise, but we never sympathise.'

Amy nodded, slightly dazed, trying to memorise his every word, thrilled that he'd grouped them together. 'You and I'. Us.

We were doing important work that might just make the world safer. Even if I was mostly taking notes and making coffee, she reminded herself with a grin as she strolled through the sleepy neighbourhood that night. She had decided to push the boat out and drop into Whole Foods to pick up dinner on the way back to her tiny dorm room. She could justify the expense on brain food.

"Scuse me, did you drop this?'

She whirled around in surprise, the Scottish accent jarring for a second.

Amy had been in the States nearly four years by then, and had deliberately softened her accent after nearly getting into a punch up with a woman in Starbucks over the pronunciation of 'raspberry yoghurt.' Her accent was far from American, but by then she could order a morning snack without a resulting chorus of *Excuse me? What did she say? Ma'am what language are you speaking?* in return.

He held out Amy's mobile phone, a little silver flip top that she thought at the time was the bee's knees. She stared at it in surprise. It had definitely been in her bag, how had she not heard it fall?

'It was on the grass,' he said as though he'd read her thoughts, pushing his glasses back up his nose. 'Must have slipped out your pocket or something.'

If Amy had seen him in a bar on a night out she doubted she would have so much as registered his presence. He was a geek long before it was chic, with a mop of messy sandy-blonde hair that another guy might have tamed with product, but he permanently looked as though he'd just leapt out of bed in surprise. Small wire rimmed glasses didn't detract from the intense blue of his eyes, though, a blue that somehow went deeper when he stared at Amy as though she were the only person on earth.

'Aye, thanks,' she muttered, and his face lit up.

'You're not Scottish as well, are you?'

'You got me,' she said with a reluctant grin.

'I'm just here for the summer.' His grin was eager, hopeful, and Amy felt her heart sinking. 'I do computery stuff, working on an Artificial Intelligence program here for a few weeks. Know in a couple of years you'll be able to walk into a coffee shop and by the time you get into the counter they'll have made your drink. Your phone will have sent them a wee signal with your usual order.'

'That right?' Amy said. 'What if you want something different that day?'

'Then you're fucked,' he replied with a grin, falling into step with her. 'See this heat, I cannae get over it.'

'You get used to it.'

'You been here long, then?'

She nodded. 'I live in Virginia most of the time at the moment. I think it's even hotter down there.'

Why was she still talking to him, she wondered. She should have taken her phone, thanked him and been half way through a quinoa wrap by now. But all of a sudden she was horribly conscious of the sheen of sweat on her forehead and shoulders.

'Jeez-o.' He was shaking his head in awe at the thought of somewhere that was even hotter than here. 'I mean, it's no' as though we don't get summer at all in Scotland. Last year it was a Tuesday.'

Amy rolled her eyes. 'That joke wasn't funny in the first century it was told,' she said, betraying her own words with a chuckle. 'I've not been home in a while,' she added.

'Then I have no choice but to buy you a drink so we can wax lyrical about pies and tablet all night then stagger home singing *Caledonia* with tears in our eyes and whisky in our hearts.'

'I hate whisky.'

He wasn't her type, Amy told herself sternly. As if she'd go for wee and nervy and keen with daft glasses in a sea of bronzed walls of muscle with tip-exed teeth and names like Brad. There was no point in getting his hopes up.

'Go on then,' Amy sighed. 'Seeing as you've got no choice.'

'Sum'dy sitting here?' The voice made Amy jump. A harassed looking young guy, gallus in jeans tight enough to leave nothing to the imagination, denim shirt clinging to well-defined muscles hovered in front of Amy as she looked up in surprise.

'Sorry, million miles away,' she muttered.

She was about to explain she was waiting for someone, but he'd already flung himself onto the sofa and was running his hands through hair gelled thickly enough to put someone's eye out.

'What's the matter with women?' he demanded suddenly.

'Men who lump us into a single monolithic entity?' Amy suggested. She turned away from his puzzled look to search again for McAvoy, a tingle of anxiety playing at the edge of her mind like the high note of a badly tuned violin. He was late. He was never late. Had the night before alerted him to something after all?

A woman tottered over to Amy's corner on heels as gravity-defying as her hair and launched into an impressive litany of Spiky-Hair's failings and he tried unsuccessfully to get Amy to defend him. *Go away the pair of you,* she silently begged, wishing she had taken the initiative to suggest they meet somewhere wee and out of the way where she could be in control. She scanned the crowd again.

If he was on to her, what would he do? Would he come after her, or would he simply move on to the next one, safe in the knowledge that she was yet to uncover anything tangible she could take to the police? Amy took another deep breath, feeling sparks of panic dance against her fingertips.

'I never done any of that!' Spiky-Hair wailed. 'I deleted it fae my phone ages ago, it's no' my fault if they keep my picture up,' he pleaded frantically. 'I've never swiped anybody in months, I love you, babe.'

'Babe' grabbed a glass of prosecco from a passing waiter and dumped it over Spiky-Hair's head, then she took off with impressive speed on her gold strappy stilts, leaving him to scarper after her.

'Think they'll make it?' Alec asked, and Amy jumped. He stood on the other side of the palm, watching as Babe grabbed an apparently random guy at the bar and started snogging the life out of him. Formerly-Spiky-Hair burst into tears.

'If those two crazy kids don't go the distance, there's no hope for the rest of us.' Amy forced a flirtatious smile, then glanced away shyly, her heart hammering. She put her glass down on the table before it slipped from her clammy hands.

Alec sat down next to her and his nearness sent a rush of something that Amy didn't care to identify fizzing through her. She must have flinched, because he shuffled back an inch or two, though he stayed close enough that she could smell his aftershave. She reached out and trailed her fingers playfully over his, praying that her fingertips weren't clammy enough to betray her.

Alec cupped her face in his hands and kissed her gently.

Amy had sat in prison interview rooms opposite dozens of men like him, chatting convivially, encouraging them, congratulating them on having eluded capture for so long as they outlined their horrific crimes, their obsessions, their need for power over life and death. She always insisted they were unshackled. They had to be. Not even the most twisted mind can feel trusted enough to open up while irons clank on their wrists and ankles. So she flirted and gasped and played to their egos, knowing all the while that if she missed a cue and they turned on her, no panic button was close enough.

It was a mask, she thought, as McAvoy started to tell her about his day in court, gesturing animatedly as he got in to the story. An exquisite, flawless mask that hid the toxic darkness festering inside. McAvoy was simply better at it than most. It was a frustration of her profession that their study of the serial killer is limited to those who have been caught: by definition, the weaker specimens.

McAvoy's mask was on active duty, purring like the engine of his fancy car with the constant fine tuning of daily social interaction, she reminded herself, watching him move confidently through the crowd towards the bar. He smiled and flirted as he ordered another round, seemingly deeply at ease with himself and the world.

The men — and one woman — Amy had interviewed, their masks were brittle, frayed, rusting. They snapped after less than an hour of questioning. Their impatience snagged through their sob stories of the terrible injustices that compelled them to slit the throat of this cashier or remove the intestines of that hairdresser, because they didn't need to pretend any more. It was all over for them. They were counting down the appeals until they were executed or died of old age waiting for it. All they had left in life was the thrill of seeing shock and revulsion in Amy's eyes before she clamped her own mask of neutral professionalism back on.

♦♦♦

Ruari polished off the last of the leftover pizza he had heated up in the microwave, and studied the card Amy had given him with her email address. Amy Kerr. His heart sank, thinking of the many billions of Amy Kerrs likely to be searchable on Google.

Sure enough, his laptop screen filled with Facebook profiles, Twitter, LinkedIn, professional websites, online articles. Ruari licked the last of the grease off his fingers and started scrolling, clicking on the odd hit that seemed promising. But over an hour later, not one hit related to the Amy he knew.

He thought for a moment then picked up the card she'd given him. *Kerr2dance110@hotmail.com*. It was obviously old, looked like the kind of address that was set up when email was just taking hold, long before it occurred to anyone that they might use them professionally. He typed it in to the search bar carefully and clicked. One hit.

It was a forum, a residents' noticeboard for what appeared to be a suburb somewhere in Texas. Frowning, he skimmed the posts. Most were from people asking if anyone knew where they could buy this or that or recommend a good local plumber. One asked for suggestions as to what gun the poster should get for her son's sixteenth birthday. Towards the bottom of the page, he found it.

Hi! My name is Amy and my husband and I have just moved into the area. We come from Scotland originally but have been living in the US for several years now. I would love to get to know our new neighbours and was wondering if there were any social gatherings or coffee mornings for residents? I can bring homemade shortbread!

Below was a handful of responses welcoming Amy to the area. Several professed Scottish heritage, one asked if she knew the McLeods in Aberdeen. One or two invited her to upcoming yoga classes and pottery workshops. Amy hadn't responded to any though, and there were no further posts from her.

Ruari got up, walked over to the window and stared down at the quiet street below. Amy was meeting McAvoy that night, he remembered. He grabbed his keys and headed for the door.

◆◆◆

He got off the subway at Buchanan Street and headed up the hill towards McAvoy's office. Bath Street was buzzing with after work drinkers. Ruari sidestepped a raucous group of guys in nearly identical grey suits smoking outside a basement bar and a couple having a shrieking fight in the middle of the road while their friends cheered them on. Three women teetered by, arm-in-arm on ankle-defying heels that made Ruari worry about whether or not they would be able to run away if necessary.

The night watchman at Alec's office building on Blythswood Square looked to be a good bit older than retirement age. He sat at a desk in the oak panelled outer office, engrossed in a book, his dark blue uniform smart and well cared for. His white hair was combed neatly but there was no taming the incongruously dark bushy eyebrows that furrowed together as he read.

Ruari stood on the pavement watching him through the glass panelled door. For over half an hour, nobody came or went, and the inner offices appeared to be in semi darkness. Finally, Ruari shoved the door open.

'I need to see Mr McAvoy.'

The security guard put down his thick book, looked at Ruari over his steel-rimmed glasses. 'You'll need to come back in the morning, son.'

'I cannae, they're gonnae arrest me, I don't know what to do.' Ruari made his voice tight and wavery, as though he were on the edge of tears. 'It wisnae my fault, I need help, man. I seen him in the papers an' I know he can help me.'

'That may well be so, but it's ten o'clock at night, he's not here.' The security guard took his glasses off, eyed Ruari as he paced agitatedly in front of him. 'Are you sure you can afford Mr McAvoy's fees, son? He doesn't come cheap.'

'I cannae go to jail, it'll kill my mother. He needs to help me, he needs to. I'm innocent, but they're gonnae stitch me up, I cannae let them.'

'Alright son, take it easy. Tell you what, why don't you take a wee seat there and I'll bring you a cup of tea. Then I'll take a few notes and have Mr McAvoy phone you first thing in the morning, okay?'

Ruari nodded and sat in one of the hardback tweed-covered chairs in the reception area. On the polished walnut coffee table in front of him was a heavy book featuring arty photographs of Scottish scenes. A Highland Cow stared solemnly at the camera from beneath her shaggy mane, the deep russet of her coat brilliant against a startlingly blue sky. Ruari couldn't help but wonder how those who actually came to McAvoy and his colleagues for help felt when they came into this office. There was a gigantic crystal bowl of purple and white flowers dotted with thistles on the ornately carved fireplace. Ruari judged it to have cost the best part of a month's wages for a lot of people who sat in this chair.

'There you are, do you take sugar?'

Ruari shook his head and took a sip of the scalding tea from a delicate china teacup. The security guard sat opposite him and opened up a spiral notebook on his lap. Somewhere outside, a siren screeched past.

'Now you understand I'm no lawyer, don't you? I can't give you any advice, I'm just gonnae take down your name and details to pass along, okay?'

'What's Mr McAvoy like?' Ruari blurted. 'Is he — will he believe me?'

'Well that's not for me to say, now is it? Why don't you write your name and —'

''I don't want to talk to him if he's just some stuck-up bugger that thinks he's better than me.'

'Mr McAvoy's no' like that.'

'How not?' Ruari demanded, dumping his tea on the gleaming coffee table. It sloshed over the side and he saw the security guard blanch. 'They floo'rs on the mantelpiece cost mair 'an ma wedding.'

'Well you wouldn't know it to look at him, but Mr McAvoy grew up in care, I'll have you know.'

Ruari's heart leapt. 'I don't believe you,' he blurted.

'That's how I got this job, his foster parents stay right next door to me and my wife. So don't you go judging him on how he looks now, he's had a hard time of it himself. Are you no' taking your tea?'

The security guard frowned, suspicion darting in his eyes. Ruari obediently picked his tea up, took a sip. 'How come?'

'How come what?'

'How come he got taken off his mum and dad?'

'He didnae get taken off them,' the security guard replied. 'His mother died, and the father wisnae on the scene. Alec was only twelve, but he was a fierce proud wee thing. Wouldn't take a scrap of pity off anyone.'

'That right?' muttered Ruari, his mind racing.

'Aye.' The security guard's chair creaked as he sat back, settled in for his tale. He glanced at Ruari's tea as though he wished he'd thought to make one for himself. 'Alec's mother saw he had brains when he was a wee boy so she wanted him to go off to some fancy school but she'd no money for it. So she went cap in hand to his father who'd no' haud a thing to do wi' him since he was made. The story went this father was a right bad bastard, a Laird of a grand estate up north somewhere. When she went to him, he ran her off his property and set the dogs on her. Wee Alec went wild at his maw when he found out. Said he didn't need a thing from a'body, and wouldn't take charity, not even from his ain faither.'

'She died not long after and the wee soul was eaten up with guilt at the way he shouted at her. He confessed it all to his foster mother when she caught him in tears in bed one night. Alec McAvoy worked his wee fingers to the bone at school and won a bursary to see him through university. That's how he became the powerful man he is today, so let that be a lesson to you, son.'

CHAPTER 7

Tuesday 11 March

Amy's chest tightened. She couldn't breathe. Image after image flew at her - dark, disturbing pictures. Women in ditches, half covered by rotting leaves, white skin stark against shadowy forest beds. Staring eyes, gaping wounds. Death, destruction, desolation. She twisted, turned, trying desperately to pull back, shrink away, close her eyes, protect herself.

Her head slammed against an unfamiliar headboard and she woke with a start. The luxurious hotel room was bathed in the half light of morning. Charcoal fittings and creamy white sheets, rumpled with her tossing and turning. She struggled to a sitting position, pulled her knees up to her chest, feeling her heart thud painfully as she tried to dislodge the sludgy dread of the dream.

Then she blinked, and bile rose in her throat. Stubble against skin, fiery lips, frantic, urgent hands gripping her hips. It all came roaring back to her, a tidal wave that took her breath away.

He was gone. She was alone. But she had got what she needed.

◆◆◆

The morning was as gloomy as dusk as Ruari half jogged up the hill to the house into which he had seen Alec

McAvoy disappear. Amy had asked him to stay away from Alec McAvoy, but she didn't say anything about his house. The pavements were covered with a thin sheen of frost, and couple of snowflakes danced in the air.

The mansion sat glowering in the shadows as Ruari approached. For a moment he thought that a tiny light was shining from within, but it was just the reflection of the headlights of a car in the driveway across the road. The driver of that car reversed over gravel then cut the engine. Ruari heard a small child's muffled yowling as footsteps crunched round to the rear door of the car. He shivered as he remembered his hallucination from the last time he was here.

Ruari considered the rusty wrought iron gates that guarded Alec McAvoy's house. A little over seven feet, he reckoned, and constructed in such a way that it was impossible to get a foothold with which to haul himself up. The property was bordered by an old wall encased in a thick hedge of rhododendrons. Ruari walked to the edge of the property searching for any break in the dense foliage large enough for him to wriggle through and over the wall, but there was none.

Back at the gates, he could just about spot a couple of patches of mossy stone on the part of the wall the property shared with the next door neighbour. It was high, but Ruari was confident he could scrabble up it with the help of the rhododendron branches, and hop over to McAvoy's property.

The gates to the neighbour's driveway were open. A gleaming black Saab sat in the driveway. The house was superficially similar to McAvoy's, but the garden was well-tended, strewn with balls, a football net, bikes of different sizes.

A conservatory had been added at the far end of the house. It was brightly lit in the dull morning, and Ruari could see a well-worn kitchen table surrounded by a gaggle of kids in school uniforms in varying states of disarray, and a toddler in pyjamas. As he watched, a harassed looking man wearing an apron over his suit came through from the kitchen carrying a large blue saucepan. He started doling out porridge into bowls, ignoring the apparent chorus of complaints.

With one eye on feeding time at the zoo, Ruari carefully made his way up their driveway keeping to the shadows. He found the gap in the rhododendrons that he'd spotted from the road, and easily hopped onto the wall. He slipped on some slick moss at the top and, swallowing a shout, landed in an ungainly heap on Alec McAvoy's driveway.

Getting to his feet, he brushed himself down and noted that the weeds on which he had fallen on were well-trampled. The darkness was cloying as he crept towards the house, he could almost taste the sense of stale neglect that thrummed in the air. After seeing that the front door was almost completely lost to thick, gnarled vines, he stole around the back, his trainers making no sound on the thick weeds and moss that suffocated the paving stones.

The back patio door lay ajar. Ruari's heart leapt into his mouth as a creak disturbed the stillness. The door swung to and fro on a gentle breeze. He could see that someone had hacked away at the foliage to gain access to the door. It had been rough and frenzied, the patio was strewn with dead leaves and branches that had been ripped away and left to rot. Not a professional job, he thought grimly, remembering how he'd initially imagined that Alec McAvoy might have bought the property to do it up and flip it for a fortune. This place wouldn't be converted with luxurious en-suite bathrooms and an open-plan kitchen with a feature Aga any time soon.

He hesitated at the edge of the patio, considering the yawning darkness that stretched deep inside the house. Other than your standard underage drinking and shop-lifting once on a dare as a teenager, Ruari had never broken the law and his every fibre bristled at the thought of entering the property. At least, he told himself it was his innate law-abiding instincts forcing him to hesitate and not the terror that was gnawing at his guts. He hadn't brought a torch, and his phone battery was running low. Finding himself plunged into pitch blackness deep in the bowels of that house was a far from appealing thought.

He needed to find a reason for the police to attend the property, he thought. Even if he did enter and find some-thing incriminating, his presence would risk putting the chain of evidence into question. Amy's words about draw-ing an airtight legal cage around McAvoy rang in his ears.

Then the patio door opened but it wasn't the wind this time. Ruari shrank back behind a huge stone birdbath and watched, hardly daring to breathe as the dark figure walked with purpose to the same spot on the wall Ruari had clambered over. He nimbly pulled himself up and disappeared into the darkness.

◆◆◆

'I feel as though I've told you everything I possibly can.'

Jen Fergusson shifted in the hard-backed, linoleum covered chair in the interview room. She forced a smile at the grim-faced officers who faced her. Jen kept forgetting the woman's name. She seemed to be in charge and had a sparky intensity about her that Jen liked; her white blonde, spiky hair put Jen in mind of a character on a children's TV show from the nineties. 'I want to do anything that will help catch him, obviously, but I just —' she took a shuddery breath. 'I also want to forget about it. If possible.'

'Of course, hopefully this will be the last time we need to interview you for the time being.' The other officer, a young guy with a shaved head and a Yorkshire accent put the tape on, marked it with the time and date and with those present. 'You definitely don't want tea or coffee?'

Jen shook her head.

'Sometimes, just going back over everything that happened a few times can help to bring out details that you've forgotten or hadn't noticed at the time,' said the female officer. Boyle, that was it. DCI Boyle. 'Memory is a funny thing, it's never quite as clear-cut or as linear as we think.'

This was the third time Jen was going over her statement, in addition to two fruitless sessions with police sketch artists. Every time she closed her eyes late at night Charlie's face loomed clear and threatening, but whenever she tried to describe him, her mind went blank and the sketches ended up laughably cartoonish. She was acutely conscious that she was the only person alive who could describe Charlie, and yet she couldn't. She forced a smile. 'Yes, of course. I understand. Please ask whatever you need to.'

'Which of you messaged first, do you remember?'

'He did. There had been something in the papers that day about NHS cuts and he asked me what I thought about it. It was a cut above the usual *hi* or *wat u up to*. I always think it's so weird people think *hi* is a conversation opener. You'd never walk up to someone at a bar or a party and just say 'hi' then stand there waiting for them to respond.'

'Never seems to occur to folk that normal social conventions still apply online,' said the guy, and Jen nodded.

'Exactly.'

'And when was this, give or take?'

'February 13th,' she replied. 'I remember that distinctly because I made some daft joke about it being just in time for Valentines, and was sure that would freak him out and he'd never reply, but he did.'

'There aren't any messages in the app on your phone prior to last Friday, the 7th of March. Did you delete them?'

Jen frowned, shook her head. 'No. No, I —' She hesitated, then shook her head again. 'I meant to, when he stopped contacting me, but I'm sure I never got around to it.' She pictured reading Charlie's message outside the chippie on Kilmarnock Road. Last Friday seemed a thousand years ago. 'Our earlier chat thread was above it when I got the new message, I'm sure of it. How could it all be deleted? Has he hacked into my phone? You've had it since Saturday morning, how is that even possible?'

All her messages. Blethers with her mum, videos of her nephew's first steps, her uni Whatsapp chat group. Her calendar. Her period tracker app. It had felt intrusive enough the thought of the police going through all of it, but the thought of Charlie reading it all that turned her stomach and for a moment she thought she might be sick.

'We're not sure yet, but if you didn't delete the messages it is a possibility,' DCI Boyle said. 'We are trying to get hold of the company behind the app to see if he could have deleted the conversation from his side. To be on the safe side, our tech team will back your phone up and secure it.'

'He would have my address if he's been in my phone.'

'A couple of officers will drive you home when we're finished and have a scout round, but try not to worry too much. So far, there is no indication of suspicious activity on your phone other than the deleted messages and it could be as simple as they automatically delete after a certain period of time. We'll know once we've spoken to the app people.'

'How difficult can it be to track them down? There must be a support email or something?'

'It's been unanswered as yet, and the physical address we found listed is in the US and essentially a PO box. Sometimes these digital startups don't have physical offices or a switchboard. They just employ remote workers all over the world, so it can be a bit tricky.'

'Right.' Jen sat back with a deep sigh. She wanted to go home and take a long bath and scour all of this from her skin with a wire sponge. But the thought of lying in the bath, naked and vulnerable, when there was even an outside chance that Charlie knew where she was, made her skin crawl.

'Can you remember what you talked about in these earlier messages? Were there many of them?'

'Hundreds. We texted round the clock for the best part of a week, and we talked about everything under the sun. Our childhoods, first loves, hopes and dreams.'

She hesitated, then shrugged. 'Sexual preferences. Fantasies, that sort of thing. Just banter. He was pretty predictable to be honest, your standard stockings, public places, threesomes. Or so he said.'

'What makes you say that?' asked Cara.

'Well, my first thought when we first met was that he was all text and no trousers. He'd been — not aggressive, exactly, over text, but quite alpha male-ish. Persistent if I was hesitant about answering something. Or if I got bored of all that *50 Shades* chat and changed the subject, he'd bring it back again and again. I suppose it was obnoxious looking back, but at the time, it seemed like a bit of a game. And it was so fast as well, messages pinging back and forth constantly, that it was a bit of a whirlwind.

'But then when we met in person, he was very different. Quite reserved, shy even. I remember thinking that if I suggested shagging in a lift in real life he would run a mile.

'Also, I know I mentioned having been travelling to Australia when we were texting. He had asked me what was the scariest thing that ever happened to me and I told him about the time I ran out of petrol when I was road tripping alone in central Queensland in the middle of nowhere. I can't remember exactly what his reply was now, but I definitely got the impression he'd been there too, or certainly had been travelling. He had this kind of knowing, 'been there done that', sort of attitude. But, at the pub I started telling a different story from my time in Oz, and he was all wide eyed impressed, like going travelling was a big deal. I thought it was sweet he'd obviously been playing the big man over text. At least —' She paused as her breath caught in her throat, forced a brief smile. 'I did at the time.'

'Did you tell him about being in training for the Tough Mudder?' asked Cara.

Jen nodded. 'Back in February, we had been making plans to meet that weekend, and I mentioned the Saturday wasn't great because I had to get up early to meet my personal trainer on the Sunday. In fact —' She frowned, remembering. 'That was when he cut off contact. I'd forgotten, but that's right. At the time I thought he just wasn't into muscles.'

◆◆◆

Ruari was grateful for the distraction of the lively group of colleagues crowding around the bar during his shift that evening. They kept one-upping each other, ordering weirder and more wonderful cocktails. Ruari had memorised the recipes for the standard Mojitos and Long Island Ice Teas and the odd retro Cosmopolitan within his first week of starting the job, but he hadn't heard of half of what they ordered. They were good sports about him following the directions in the dog-eared cocktail bible that was kept under the bar, encouraging him with raucous cheers when he set an orange peel alight and nearly took half his fingertip with it.

They were a digital marketing team, he was informed several times by several people, celebrating winning a big pitch after weeks of tumbleweed on the work front. The managing director, his curly grey hair worn long, the broken capillaries over his nose marring an otherwise crinkly handsomeness, drunkenly confided that the agency was on its last legs. Ruari couldn't help thinking that the bar tab wasn't going to help much. He'd been bantering with them for well over an hour before he noticed that the creative director, her long blonde hair ironed straight, in a skin-tight black dress that showed off many dedicated hours in the gym, was watching him more than strictly necessary. He blushed and she chuckled. He tripped over his own feet and dropped the cocktail shaker.

It wasn't until he knelt to sweep up the scattered ice cubes that it hit him he hadn't thought of Lorna since the digital marketers came in and a hot wave of guilt swept over him. He studiously avoided the creative director's gaze for the rest of the evening, though within minutes she was sitting on the lap of a furiously blushing twenty-something work experience guy.

The digital marketing crew finally stormed off in search of some dancing by just after eleven and Ruari wondered if he could get away with ringing the last orders bell a quarter of an hour early. The kitchen shut early on weeknights and he felt restless, trapped. He scanned the occupied tables with a practiced eye, judged that the couple holding hands in the corner would be content with the nearly half a bottle of red on their table. Three middle aged woman by the window had drained their bottle of prosecco but were killing themselves laughing over some funny story or other. He reckoned they wouldn't bother ordering again, and was about to poke his head round the office door to ask if he could start shutting up the bar when he spotted her.

Kerry. Lorna's friend from her journalism class was sitting with a group of people in a booth in the far corner. Ruari had met Kerry once when he and Lorna had run into her and some pals at one of their post-Crossfit drinks sessions. He remembered that she'd evidently picked up something about the way he looked at Lorna, because she spent the whole night giving him drunken thumbs up while he prayed she wouldn't slur anything incriminating out loud.

She glanced up as he looked over, and Ruari had a sneaking suspicion she had been waiting for him to notice her. He slung his dish towel over his shoulder and went over to the table, gathered up a couple of empty glasses before finally meeting Kerry's eye.

'Still can't really believe it,' she blurted without preamble. She shook her head. 'Sorry. Such a cliché. It's amazing how many you come out with when something like this happens. She was so young, everything to live for, such a waste.'

Kerry smiled with shining eyes and Ruari glanced around the restaurant, willing one of the other customers to call him over.

'Oh God I really miss her,' said Kerry. 'I nearly jacked this course in because it's so bloody horrible walking into the classroom, looking for her then remembering she'll never be there again. Only thing that stops me is I know fine she'll haunt me if I don't get my diploma. The one cliché that is a load of shite is the one about it getting easier as time passes. Takes your breath away, sometimes, how much you miss her, doesn't it?'

She poured out all of this in one breath, her eyes filling with tears. Ruari stared at the floor, as she blinked them away impatiently. 'Sorry, I hate being so pathetic. I keep thinking, if I feel like this, what must her family be going through?'

Ruari nodded again, not quite trusting himself to speak.

'It's just I feel so guilty too,' she added. 'I mean it was my fault. What was I thinking?'

'It wasn't your fault,' he muttered around the hard lump forming in his throat. 'How could it be your fault?'

Kerry wiped her eyes with the back of her hand. 'I don't know what I was playing at. She kept saying that online dating wasn't her style, she wasn't interested, but I just thought she was never going to meet someone otherwise so I kept on insisting. I didn't even know she'd done it until I read in the papers that's how she met her killer and I just —' Her words were engulfed by a shaky sob. She took a deep breath, forced herself under control. 'I don't know how single people do it these days, it all just seems so difficult. I just wanted someone to appreciate her, you know?'

Ruari picked up the glasses he hadn't noticed he'd put down, a muscle in his jaw working overtime.

'The mad thing is, I was sure she'd met somebody. We do a presentation of what we're working on at our Friday night class, and that week, Lorna wouldn't present. She said she'd not had a chance to work on anything, but it wasn't like her and I was so sure she had spent the time all cosy with some man, and I was going to ask her about it at the next class on the Tuesday, but —'

'I need to get back,' Ruari blurted. A raging whitewater coursed through him, threatened to smash his composure to smithereens at any moment. 'Boss is just in the office, she'll have my guts for garters if she sees me blethering.'

'Aye, sorry, don't mind me banging on. Ruari, isn't it? You were a good pal to her, I know. She thought the world of you.'

'Lorna was not on those apps to date,' slurred a tall guy with striking hair as white blonde as a baby's. He slumped next to Kerry, his pint half dangling from his hand as he tried to focus.

'What was she on them for then?' Kerry demanded. 'Looking for a squash partner?'

'It was for a story,' said the drunk guy, and Ruari thought he detected an accent. German maybe?

'She never said anything about a story on internet dating to me.'

The German shrugged and took another slurp of his pint. 'She was writing a story about the return of Jack the Ripper,' he grinned. 'There was a series of unsolved murders in London some years ago and the killer disappeared like that.' He clicked his fingers. 'Into thin air. He met his victims through dating apps, so Lorna downloaded a couple of them just to understand how they work, to see if he could have targeted specific women or was it random. The Dancing Girl Murders they called them, in London.'

♦♦♦

'The whole thing is SUCH a load of shite,' Kelly Gallagher laughed as she peered into her wee bedroom mirror and applied another coat of mascara to her false lashes. Her cousin, Ann Marie, put her feet up on Kelly's bedside table and struggled to reach round her bump to paint her toenails. Ann Marie had married at twenty and was now pregnant with her third, so she didn't have the first clue about the total hellishness that was dating in the modern world, in Kelly's considered opinion.

'See these chancers right, their profiles are all full of, *if you're into drama, if your photies are a' duck faces, if you look like a different person under a' that slap, jist swipe on*. I'm like, I'll bloody swipe whatever way I want, pal. An' the worst ones —' Satisfied with her eyes, she moved on to selecting a lip liner from her professional-grade makeup box. 'Are they ones that give you instructions on basic human inter-actions. *If we match, say hi.* Naw, if we match I'll just panic and throw my phone in the Clyde. *If you like the look of me, swipe right.* I'd never've thought o' that if you'd not told me! *Just looking to date and see how things go* — as opposed to WHIT? As opposed to, if you don't warn me aff I'll just rock up in a wedding dress and be like, right you an' me, pal. Boom. Job done. Oh you just wanted to meet me an' see how things go? You should've said.'

'Oh give them a break, they're just trying to be friendly,' muttered Ann Marie. 'You shouldnae be so hard on folk.'

'How no'? If they're wantin' a shot at all this —' She gestured to her curvy figure and Ann Marie laughed. 'They can just step up their game.'

Three weeks previously, Kelly had walked in to her local to find her fiancé Mike winching the face off the barmaid, who was barely eighteen and, in Kelly's opinion, looked as though she should set phone reminders to breathe in and out. Kelly had turned and walked right back out and grabbed a baseball bat from under her nephew's bed.

Within an hour she'd battered the hell out of the white van Mike used for his window cleaning business and downloaded Tinder.

Mike had called the police for destruction of property, but when Kelly explained the situation to the two female officers who attended, they decided the windscreen could easily have been smashed to smithereens because he had been driving without due care and attention and gave him a ticket instead.

Mike had since got Kelly's name tattooed across his chest in an effort to win her back, but she'd already sold her engagement ring on eBay and booked a holiday with Ann Marie with the proceeds. Truth was, she'd been bored out her bonkers by Mike for years. He'd done her a favour.

She'd been having the time of her life ever since, cheerfully burning her way through every dating app available, laughing in the face of most chancers before lecturing them on why they were single and swanning out out the pub leaving them with the bill.

Fire engine red, she thought with satisfaction, lining her lips flawlessly before reaching for the Chanel lipstick that was her pride and joy. This Charlie guy seemed a bit of a wee lost soul, she thought. She'd put a bit of whisky in his willy and send him on his way.

'Would ye no' just go back to Mike?' Ann Marie asked for the thirty-five thousandth time. 'Everybody's got their outfits for the wedding, it seems an awfy shame.'

'Ach yese can wear yer ootfits when he marries that halfwit fae the pub,' Kelly replied, blowing herself a kiss in the mirror. 'He was never good enough for me, which should be your line to me and no' the other way around, by the way.'

'I just think it's time you settled down Kelly, you're nearly thirty. You know what happens to a woman's fertility after —'

'Och get tae,' Kelly laughed, kissing the top of her sister's head and nicking her good purse. 'See you later, pet, don't wait up.'

◆◆◆

Less than an hour later, Ruari hovered just out of sight of the main entrance of Alec McAvoy's chambers. The security guard was deep in his book again and didn't look up. It was a clear night and the square was bathed in the silvery glow of the moon.

The German had insisted that everything Lorna had been working on was in her blog, that it was the police's job to work out if any of it was relevant, not his. He'd shrugged defensively when Ruari snapped that he couldn't assume anything, that he had to report anything Lorna had talked about. The group had gone quiet when Ruari stormed off, but it wasn't until he saw the women with the prosecco looking over in alarm that he realised how loudly he had shouted. He suspected he was no longer employed and couldn't quite find it within himself to care.

Ruari could see a single lamp on in the office just to the left of the reception area. He was fairly confident that office was McAvoy's. When the security guard was telling Ruari about McAvoy the other night, he had unconsciously gestured towards that door once or twice.

After a few moments, a figure came to that window and looked out, a troubled expression playing on his features. Ruari's breath caught in his throat. It was McAvoy.

Ruari stepped behind a nearby parking meter and pretended to count out some change in his hand. He half turned his back to the window even though there were no streetlights nearby. He was safe in the darkness.

McAvoy retreated from the window and Ruari crouched in front of the wrought iron fence surrounding the square, shielded from view behind a large hunting green Range Rover. He pulled out the wee spiral bound notebook he'd picked up in a corner shop, noted the time and location he'd spotted McAvoy, and settled down on the pavement to wait. He couldn't see all of the office window, but he would be alerted if the lights went out.

Ruari pulled up his hood, grateful he was wearing his oldest, shabbiest windbreaker, and hunkered down as though trying to sleep. He wasn't sure how much time had passed before he saw McAvoy's office go dark as he was afraid of risking the glow of his phone on the off-chance someone noticed it. Adrenaline pierced his guts as he spotted McAvoy's familiar silhouette making his way down the steps of his office.

'Och that's terrible, a young boy like you? Can you no' get a job, son?' Ruari blinked into the concerned face of an elderly man. Craning his neck, Ruari spied McAvoy heading in the direction of Bath Street.

'Here —' The old man pressed a pound coin into Ruari's hand. 'Have yourself a wee cup of tea, okay?'

'No I — you're alright, I'm really —'

Ruari got to his feet and started backing away, frantically trying to keep an eye on McAvoy who was walking briskly down the hill.

'Go back to school if you can, son. You only get one life.'

'… thanks very much.'

The man patted Ruari's hand, closing it around the pound coin, then shuffled off leaning heavily on his walking stick. Ruari waited a moment then turned and sprinted after McAvoy.

He caught him at the pedestrian crossing at Hope Street and shrank back to hover next to a basement bar from which a heavy bass thudded, staring unseeingly at the menu. McAvoy turned right on Buchanan Street and wound his way through the throng of late night shoppers before turning left towards George Square. There was a percussion band playing in front of the subway station - a group of massive bearded guys in kilts drumming an urgent, tribal beat. The beat matched Ruari's heartbeat as he sidestepped wee old ladies and buggies and a crowd of teenaged goths shrieking with laughter.

He risked following a little more closely behind McAvoy in the crowd, afraid that he might hop on a train at Queen Street station and he would lose him. But McAvoy turned right to cross George Square. Ruari slipped behind the statue of Sir Walter Scott when a flurry of horns and shouts on Queen Street caused McAvoy to glance back. Finally, he disappeared into a fancy members' club on a wee alleyway off Ingram Street.

◆◆◆

'I'm really sorry, my boss is not answering her phone and our client in the States is doing his nut trying to reach her. I'll be really quick, I promise.' The flawlessly made up receptionist flashed Ruari a smile that hinted at several thousand pounds worth of dental work. 'She'll tear a strip off me if I don't get hold of her the night.'

'No bother,' the receptionist said. 'I know what it's like. Just poke your head in there and try not to lower the tone too much, eh?'

Ruari grinned and headed to where she pointed. It was a small dining room, with leather club chairs and floor-to-ceiling bookcases stuffed with venerable old books. Ruari crossed to the bar and nodded to the barman, perusing the cocktail menu as he scanned the room through the mirrored wall behind the bar. Alec McAvoy was in the far corner at a table covered in green felt, with a group of men who might as well have had Very Important stamped across their foreheads. One was carefully trimming a cigar, his tailored three-piece pinstripe suit stretched over a substantial gut. A white-gloved waiter brought a dusty bottle of whisky to the table on a silver tray surrounded by crystal tumblers. The man in the pinstripe suit handed the tumblers round. McAvoy accepted his without breaking stride on the animated story he was telling a younger man with a prominent Adam's apple.

Ruari handed the menu back to the barman and slipped out.

'Did you get her okay?' asked the receptionist as he walked past.

'Wisnae there,' he replied cheerfully, stepping out into the night. 'I reckon she's having an affair.'

On the way home, he bought himself a packet of Smarties with the old man's pound.

CHAPTER 8

Wednesday 12 March

When Lina Olofsson was nineteen, she fell head over heels in love with Jimmy Finnegan while Inter-Railing across the Austrian Alps in 1957. He had hair the colour of fire, a habit of developing an urgent need to answer a call of nature whenever the ticket inspector appeared, and he made her laugh until her tummy hurt. When they reached Budapest, she wired her family in Norrtälje to say that she was moving to Scotland. They were married at Govan Parish Church three weeks later.

Children had never happened, but they had been happy, she thought with a deep sigh. She yawned. Her beloved Yorkie Hedvig sniffed happily around the abandoned rec area behind her flat and Lina tucked her hand-knitted scarf snuggly into her cardigan and shivered.

She really should have taken Hedvig to Cathkin Braes today, she thought guiltily. Hedvig only demanded to go out in the middle of the night like this when she'd not had a good run during the day, but Lina's knees had been playing up something awful and the lift in the tower block was broken again. By the time she finally accepted Hedvig wasn't going to let her go back to sleep it was nearly midnight. She had put on several layers of cardigans over her nightie and creaked her way down seven flights of stairs and across the graffiti-strewn yard to the open ground.

The ground used to be the site of another tower block, the twin of her own, but it had been condemned and knocked down some time in the late nineties when Jimmy was first going downhill. There was talk of a community play park, and several lively meetings had been held when residents voted on a fish pond and swing set. Colin Murchison made everyone laugh when he announced he'd never seen a fish that 'wisnae covered in vinegar.' But cuts meant the park never materialised and Colin Murchison was yet to bear witness to an un-battered fish. Over the years the ground had become an unofficial dump, strewn with rusty buggies, a hopelessly bent whirly, the occasional used needle, a set of mouldy garden furniture often used as a meeting place by local kids and one, inexplicable, eight foot tall stuffed stag.

It occasionally occurred to Lina that she really should be nervous, an old lady doddering about in the middle of the night on dodgy knees in one of the most notorious areas of Glasgow. Hedvig was firmly useless on the protection front. The one time some daft punk tried to mug her three or four years ago, Hedvig had jumped up to lick his knees, nearly wagging her wee bum off in her excitement. As luck would have it, it unnerved him so much he scarpered anyway, but it was a trick unlikely to work twice.

But this was Lina's bit. Everyone knew her. The local criminals paused their shootouts to serenade her with *Dancing Queen* as she and Hedvig shuffled by.

Lina hadn't returned to Sweden or spoken a word of Swedish in over sixty years, but recently, she had caught herself speaking Swedish in her head to herself. She wondered if it was a sign that her body sensed it was nearing the end, that it was returning to its roots. She wondered if she could afford a flight to Stockholm. She would like to smell the Baltic Sea one last time. And eat a warm, sticky *kanelbulle* straight from the oven. What was that in English again, she thought irritably.

Ahh fy fan, she thought as she laid eyes on the woman carelessly dumped amongst the buggies and a shopping trolley. Her pale skin glowed silver in the moonlight, dark eyes stared unseeingly back at Lina. She was so perfectly made up she looked like a doll, though her bright red lipstick looked almost black in the darkness. Hedvig yapped around the woman, snuffling at her as though in an attempt to wake her up.

'*Kom hit, Hedvig,*' Lina snapped, her eyes filling up. '*Hon kommer aldrig vakna igen. Stackars tjej.*'

She turned and scurried as fast as her knees would take her home to phone the police. She was wheezing her way up the third flight of stairs when it finally popped into her head.

Cinnamon bun.

◆◆◆

Ruari had woken early with a notion to make himself some nourishing lentil soup. He was than a little proud of himself for remembering his Granny's recipe. As he waited for the lentils to soften before adding the chopped root veggies, he had a scroll through social media on his phone.

On Facebook a predictable group of friends were going round in their usual pointless circles over Independence on a post by the Scottish National Party. His sister-in-law had uploaded a video of his ten-year-old niece Highland dancing, and Ruari clicked to 'like' it. Aoife O'Brien was in a relationship. Not entirely proud of the way his heart lurched, Ruari clicked on his ex-girlfriend's page. His replacement's profile picture showed him standing on top of some mountain or another, ropes and harnesses clipped to his waist, his arms raised in triumph. Aoife had commented on the photo, an entire row of heart emojis. Her comment was dated less than a month after their split. *Good for her,* thought Ruari grimly as he clicked to unfriend her.

It was then that he saw that Dancing Girl Murders was trending. Heart sinking, he clicked on the first link and watched with growing horror a video of the wee old lady with the soft lilting accent haltingly describe how she found the body late the night before.

'*Hon — hon såg så vacker ut,* in the moonlight,' the old lady said, her voice cracking, a wee yappy dog snuffling around her lap. 'Like a doll. I almost thought she would start to turn around as a lullaby played like in a little girl's jewellery box.' She then mumbled something under her breath, looking confused and distressed. The screen went blank.

The victim's name was Kelly Gallagher. A photo of flashed up on the screen, grinning and making a peace sign at the camera, squinting against the sunshine at what looked like a festival. She had been found posed in a ballet position.

Forgetting to turn the heat down on the soup so that it could simmer gently, Ruari wandered through to the living room and picked up a black marker. Grimly noting it was lucky he hadn't got around to decorating yet, he wrote *Kelly Gallagher* directly on the living room wall, circled it and drew lines connecting her to Lorna, Jen Fergusson, Kerry Matheson, Amina Rashid and Maja Nilsson. Underneath each of their names he had scribbled notes and thoughts and questions, and he now balanced his phone on the bookshelf perpendicular to the wall so he could copy out the details discovered so far about Kelly Gallagher.

Enterprising journalists had already found her dating app profile. In one of the photos she was cheerfully chopping her wedding dress to pieces, grinning maniacally at the camera. It occurred to Ruari that she and Lorna would have got on.

Charlie.

Kelly Gallagher's sister reported that she was going on a date that night with a man named Charlie. That was the same name reported by Jen Fergusson and Amina Rashid's flatmate.

Ruari stepped back from the wall, tapping the marker against his teeth as he took it all in.

Lorna went for a drink with Alec McAvoy, he thought. That was undisputed, he'd seen it with his own eyes. The next night McAvoy took part in a web conference for the rest of the night. Lorna went out to meet somebody else — Charlie? — and was found the following morning in the Campsies, near where she used to play as a child.

Two nights later, Jen Fergusson finally went on a date with a guy named Charlie with whom she had been messaging on and off for weeks. He tried to attack her and she escaped. The following night, Kelly Gallagher went on a date with a Charlie she had also met on a dating app and was found dead later that night.

Knowing it would be too good to be true, Ruari opened his laptop and Googled

Alec Charles McAvoy
Alexander Charles McAvoy
Charles Alexander McAvoy
Charles McAvoy barrister
Nothing.

He flopped back on the sofa, then winced in pain, wondering if he would ever remember just how absurdly unyielding it was prior to flinging himself onto it. He would replace it as soon as he got a new job, he promised himself. Some day.

Then he sat up again, thought for a second before searching

Dancer murder Glasgow
Glasgow ballet murder

Halfway down the page, he spotted a hit that looked promising. It was an old article from the *Glasgow Herald* archives, about a murder of a nurse who had worked at Stobhill Hospital. The murder took place almost exactly twenty years previously, and while it remained unsolved, police believed that Elaine MacPherson was the victim of a mugging gone wrong. The article mentioned in passing that as a child Elaine had trained to be a ballerina at the Royal Ballet School in Richmond Park in London.

That was where the three victims in London were found, Ruari thought, wondering if there could possibly be a connection. But Jen Fergusson had described Charlie as being in his late twenties or early thirties. It wasn't likely he had been involved in a murder twenty years ago.

Ruari shut the laptop again and sighed. His brain felt sluggish and useless, disparate thoughts trundling pointlessly in circles. He looked up at his mind-map wall, his scribbles swimming before his exhausted eyes. After a moment or two his gaze came to rest on the note he had made under Kelly Gallagher's name and his blood ran cold.

12:17am body found off Castlemilk Road by Lina Olofsson
That couldn't be right.

He grabbed his jacket from where he had tossed it on the doorknob of the hallway cupboard when he had got home the night before, and rummaged in the pocket for his wee notebook.

11:52 office in Blythswood Square

12:07 private members' club - Ingram Street

He pulled up the article that included a bullet point rundown of the information the police had received so far.

Kelly Gallagher had not been dead an hour when she was found.

Even if McAvoy had killed her at 11:18 on the dot and jumped in a car or managed to hail a taxi within minutes, it had to be a twenty-minute drive from where Kelly Gallagher was found to where Ruari had seen McAvoy with his own two eyes in his office on Blythswood Square. And Ruari had been standing outside the office for at least five or ten minutes before he spotted McAvoy at the window.

It wasn't possible.

Either the police were mistaken —

Or Ruari was McAvoy's alibi.

◆◆◆

'There's a professional translator on her way from Edinburgh,' said Ricky, hanging up the phone.

Cara nodded. 'I don't want to keep her here any longer than absolutely necessary. She told the first on scene officers she could speak English, but she keeps switching to Swedish halfway through sentences.'

Stellan sat across the room with Lina Olofsson, speaking softly with her.

'*Min mormors kanelbullen är de bästa i världen,*' he was saying, patting her hand. '*Jag är säker på att någon tar hand om Hedvig, men jag ska kolla med min fru, okej?*'

'*Är hon din fru? Så snygg hon är!*'

Stellan looked up as Cara and Ricky took their seats opposite them.

'She wants to know if somebody is taking care of her dog,' he said. 'She also says that you are beautiful.'

'Some officers took the dog for a walk this morning, and there's someone at the flat with her just now,' said Ricky. Cara grinned, subtly rolling her eyes at Stellan.

'She also says that she saw a man she did not know walking away from the park as she and Hedvig walked towards it. *Kommer du ihåg exact vad klockan var?*'

'*Midnatt, ungefärr,*' replied Lina.

'Midnight,' said Cara with a smile.

'My little dog would not let me get back to sleep. I should have walked her in the day,' Lina said hesitantly.

'Can you remember what the man looked like at all?'

Lina thought a moment, then mumbled in Swedish to Stellan.

'About my height,' he said.

'Quite tall for a Glaswegian,' commented Ricky.

'She thinks dark hair and eyes, and a sharp face like a crow, though he had a straight nose.'

'I think you say skinny malinky long legs,' said Lina, and Cara smiled.

'He was alone?'

Lina nodded.

'Thank you,' said Cara. 'Tack.'

The professional translator arrived then, and Cara arranged for Lina to give her official statement to Ricky and Samira. She stood outside the interview for a few moments, deep in thought.

'Are you okay?' asked Stellan.

'It's the oddest thing. I felt it when Jen Fergusson described him, I got the weirdest sensation that the description sounded familiar, like I know someone that fits it.' She shook her head helplessly.

Stellan leaned down and kissed her forehead.

'I'll make dinner,' he said.

'I'll do my best to eat it,' she replied.

'Yeah, yeah, I believe that when I see it.' His laughter echoed down the hallway and Cara stood there a few more moments once he'd left, wracking her brains.

◆◆◆

An acrid smell filled the flat and Ruari realised that he had burned the soup. He bolted into the kitchenette and dumped the smoky, stinking mess in the sink and wondered ruefully if the sausages he was fairly confident were in the freezer counted towards his health kick. Deciding they were better than nothing, he opened the freezer and his heart lurched.

Fanny.

Lorna.

He started to laugh and grabbed the note, held it to his face, knowing fine no sense of her would remain after several weeks in the freezer. Feeling grateful for a wee boost from Lorna before he broke the news to Amy that McAvoy was innocent, he turned the note over in his hands and that's when he saw the phone number.

◆◆◆

'Castlemilk, man? Are you sure?' The taxi driver looked dubiously at Ruari as he jumped in the back.

'Just swing by quickly then on to the city centre. You don't even need to slow down.'

'Aye well if you're sure.' The taxi swung in such a startling U-turn that Ruari was slammed against the window.

'Whereabouts exactly?'

Ruari read out the address of the rec ground where Kelly Gallagher was found.

'Ah know what happened there,' the taxi driver said as the taxi trundled through the Clyde Tunnel. 'Ah seen it in the papers. Pure tragic. You're not some pervert rubber-necker, are you?'

Ruari shook his head. 'I'm a journalist,' he said, watching the cats eyes flash by in the darkness of the tunnel. When he was wee, his Granny told him that he had to hold his breath going under a bridge so as not to disturb the fairies that lived there. Weeks later, he'd nearly passed out in the back of the car just about where the taxi was now, trying to hold his breath all the way through the long tunnel.

'Oh aye, for one of the big papers?'

'I can't really say. Undercover,' he improvised wildly.

'That right? They're a' crooks and criminals, you know. Murdered Princess Di.'

'Sorry about that,' said Ruari as they popped back up into daylight and tower blocks appeared on the horizon.

Half an hour later, Ruari ended the stopwatch on his phone. He paid the driver, adding a generous tip, and stepped out onto Blythswood Square. Twenty-three minutes. There was no way McAvoy could have done it any faster.

◆◆◆

'The discovery of this body concerns me deeply for two reasons.'

There was a palpable buzz in the air as Gerry Forsyth, the forensic psychologist Cara had asked to consult on the investigation, addressed the packed meeting in his haughty Edinburgh accent. Gerry looked like the indulgent uncle who'd slip you a beer when you were twelve, Cara thought, in his crumpled cheap navy suit, salt and pepper combover and kind grey eyes. He spoke softly and it was as though the room held its collective breath so as to catch every word. Cara once asked him if he deliberately lowered his voice to force people to lean forward to hear him, but he'd just chuckled.

'The decreasing length of time between attacks, and the frenzied nature of it. If you look here —' He pointed to the projection on the whiteboard, a timeline of the three London murders and the three Glasgow attacks.

'Three months between Kerry Matheson's death and Amina Rashid's, then ten weeks elapsed until Maja Nilsson died. This time around, the timeline is much more compact. This time the gap between deaths is days. Part of the definition of a serial killer is that they have a cooling off period between their crimes, sometimes lasting as long as years. This is in contrast with a spree killer, who murders several people at once or within a very short time period, such as a mass shooter or a suicide bomber. However, it is not uncommon for serial killers to escalate, like any addict. Each individual kill satisfies them less and less, until they go on a final spree. This is the pattern that we could be seeing here.'

A sense of horror filled the room like tear gas.

'Can we put out a public warning, get people to stay at home?' Ricky asked.

'What about the nature of the attack?' asked Cara. She'd had the same thought about a public warning, but worried it could turn into pandemonium with vigilantes whacking anyone they fancied had the look of a serial killer.

'If you look here —' Gerry clicked on his laptop, and an image of Kelly Gallagher's body lying on the medical examiner's slab filled the whiteboard. 'Kelly Gallagher was strangled and posed in ballet's fifth position, just like the others, so she broadly fits the pattern. However, if you compare her to the other victims — '

He clicked to open up photographs of the other four women. 'You can see that there is significantly more bruising, both around her neck and on her face and elsewhere on her body, suggesting that she was handled more roughly, possibly knocked to the ground before he began to strangle her. The other kills are more controlled, more measured. "Neat" for want of a better word, in comparison.'

'Could it be because she fought back?' Ricky asked. Cara noticed that Samira hadn't said a thing yet. She was watching Gerry suspiciously from the back of the room, though she did appear to be taking notes.

'There are significant defensive wounds on her hands and fingers,' Gerry said. 'But that is the case with some of the others and it doesn't seem to have fazed him before. He seems less in control this time, less sure of himself, and there is more of a sense of brute force. The fact that she was left on open waste ground while the others were carefully placed in more remote, heavily wooded areas supports this further. It was risky. While the rec area where she was found isn't well-lit, it is overlooked by several tower blocks, plus two of the three ways to reach it involve passing busy pubs that would have been chucking out around that time. He doesn't normally take these kinds of risks.'

'What about a copycat, or someone who wanted to kill Kelly Gallagher for their own reasons and make it look as though she is one of this killer's victims?' asked Ricky.

'Jensen and I spoke to her fiancé,' a young DI whose name Cara wasn't sure of piped up. 'They had quite the acrimonious split and she totalled his car, but he was in the pub all night last night. There was an Old Firm game on and when Celtic scored he striped naked and did the running man, so a fair few witnesses clearly recalled seeing him.'

'We also haven't publicised the specifics of the ballet positions,' added Cara. 'The press know that they are something to do with dancing, but not that they go in this sequence of first position and so on. It seems unlikely anybody else would have known to pose her like that.'

'And assuming it's the same guy, my opinion is that he is unravelling, and fast.' Gerry nodded. 'There is something else. Kelly Gallagher also represents a departure from the victim profile. Every one of the other victims were educated, professional, ambitious. Kelly Gallagher was enrolled on a psychology degree at Strathclyde University and due to start later this year, but was at the time employed as a cleaner. According to the messages we found on her phone between her and Charlie, she never mentioned her upcoming course.'

'Lorna Stewart was a hotel receptionist.'

'That's true, but as she does not appear to have used the dating apps - it is possible he initially found her through this missing blog of hers, so thought of her as a journalist. The tone of his messages to Kelly Gallagher is quite different too. If you look at this string of messages with Jen Fergusson —' Gerry clicked to open up a new slide. 'Jen wrote out as many as she could recall for us, and the phrasing matches what the screengrabs Kerry Matheson saved of her messages with him. His tone is teasing, flirtatious. He drew each of them cleverly into admitting vulnerabilities in a playful way with the game of Truth or Dare. It is both extremely manipulative, and patient. However with Kelly Gallagher, he is much more aggressive, insistent, daring her to meet with him the following night. *I thought you said you were brave?* He is throwing down a gauntlet within a day of establishing contact with her, which again, is a departure from his previous methodology.'

'Could it be that he alters his approach depending on the woman he is trying to seduce?' Ricky cringed at his choice of words, then continued. 'From what we have gathered so far about Kelly Gallagher, she seemed particularly ballsy and daring, maybe he sensed she would respond to that sort of aggression?'

'Very good point, and it could well be the case,' said Gerry slowly. 'I'd like to do some more analysis on these messages,' he added looking at Cara who nodded.

'I don't see how it's going to help us catch him,' blurted Samira sharply. 'Look I'm sorry, but — yakking on about the way he goes about chatting up his victims doesn't exactly help us come up with a name, does it?'

'My job is simply to provide some insight where I can into his actions,' said Gerry. 'I'm not a magician or a psychic, all I can do is help you draw patterns that might just assist in —'

'DCI Boyle?' Everyone looked up as a young woman in uniform poked her head around the door. 'Good news from the lab. He left some DNA behind this time. They've asked if you can come down right away.'

◆◆◆

'Look —' Amy fumbled in her bag, brought out something wrapped in a plastic sandwich bag. 'I don't have much time. Could you do me a favour? The police have the killer's DNA now. You must know someone in the lab who could test it.'

Amy glanced around to make sure no one was paying them any attention as Ruari took the bag and unravelled it just enough to see what it was. A toothbrush. A plain white one, the kind you get on planes or from hotels if you've forgotten yours. Amy met his eye with a defensive glare.

'McAvoy used it,' she said.

The bell over the door dinged and a flustered young woman came in, pushing a buggy that screeched and wailed. The dreadlocked girl from behind the counter told a couple of students at a corner table to beat it so the woman could sit down. They shrugged and complied, and the young mum sat and started to breastfeed the wriggling, screaming creature that emerged from the buggy with a grateful smile.

'How do you know the police have the killer's DNA?' he asked. 'I've not seen that in any of the papers.'

He wasn't sure if he imagined the flicker of hesitation in Amy's expression. 'I have a source,' she said.

'On DCI Boyle's team?'

'It's better for you not to know details.'

'But I'm expected to help you while you keep me in the dark?'

'I thought it was about helping Lorna.'

Ruari flinched, looked away. 'If I did know someone, where are they supposed to say they got this?' he asked after a moment, turning the toothbrush in its plastic bag over in his hands. Kevin MacGregor's boyfriend Jack worked in the lab, he knew. Ruari didn't know Jack well, but knew he would do a favour if Kevin asked. 'There are systems, everything is logged. You can't just slip a bit of extra evidence into the pile.'

'He couldn't do a bit of overtime, run the tests when no one else is around?'

'That's asking a lot.'

'Ruari if you don't want to get involved I understand. This kind of work isn't for everyone, it involves risks and it involves making people uncomfortable. I can approach Jack myself if you prefer.'

'What was your maiden name?'

If Amy was startled by the sudden change of subject, she didn't show it. 'Kerr has always been my name,' she said.

'Why aren't you online anywhere?'

'I like to keep a low profile.'

Ruari noted she didn't comment on the fact he had searched for her. It was unnerving the way nothing surprised her.

'I deal with a lot of dangerous people,' she explained. 'I've had clients follow me home, convicts my testimony helped put away try to track me down. And more importantly, as a psychologist it's important to come across as neutral as possible. What if somebody came to me because of an abusive, traumatic relationship then found happy family photos of me with a loving husband and kids online? Do you think she would feel as comfortable opening up to me if she felt as though I had what she didn't?'

Ruari finished his coffee, putting the mug down with more force than he had intended. The rickety table wobbled.

'Alec McAvoy didn't kill Kelly Gallagher,' he said.

'What makes you think that?'

'He can't have. I was following him that night. There wasn't time for him to get from where she died to where I saw him. I checked it.'

'That's not possible.'

'And yet it is.'

'Were you working?' Amy asked.

Ruari nodded.

'Last orders is quarter past eleven, the bar shuts at half eleven, right? Then what? You wipe down the tables, put clean glasses away, cash out the till?'

'It was quiet that night, none of that took long.'

'Even so, how could you have your eyes on McAvoy much before midnight?'

'I checked the time,' Ruari snapped. 'I'm not a halfwit.'

'On your phone?'

'My watch. I didn't want to get my phone out in the dark.'

'So you looked at your watch in the dark, can you be certain you saw the exact right time?'

'I've been telling the time for quite a few years.'

'I'm just saying Ruari, when it comes to Alec McAvoy you have to be surer than sure. We've got one chance to get him and if we screw it up it's all over, for good. Even though a DNA match from this toothbrush wouldn't be admissible, it could be compelling enough to be able to hand over to the police. Isn't that what you've wanted all along? This could be the break we have been waiting for. But if you don't want to get involved —'

'I am involved,' Ruari said shortly, staring at the plastic wrapped toothbrush in his hand. 'But —'

'But what?'

'How do you know?'

'How do I know what?'

'That he is the killer.'

'I can't tell you everything,' Amy said slowly. She didn't break eye contact and Ruari started to feel uncomfortable under her scrutiny.

'If you want me to help, you need to tell me something.'

Amy nodded. 'Fair enough.

'McAvoy was interviewed in London by the Metropolitan Police five years ago,' she began. 'I told you that. They traced a bunch of flowers sent to the first victim, Kerry Matheson, to him. He'd used his own credit card, but of course he had an alibi for the time of her murder. He was at a Law Society dinner, confirmed by dozens of the country's finest legal minds. Who, by the time of Kerry's death, were so drunk they couldn't have picked their mothers out of a lineup.

"Kerry?' Amy imitated McAvoy's imperious Kelvinside accent. The venom in her voice made Ruari uneasy. *'Oh yes of course, blonde, pretty? We went out once, I took her for dinner at that 1920s speakeasy place by Old Street. I think I came on a bit strong with the flowers afterwards, I never heard from her again. You win some, you lose some.* He actually said that. You win some you lose some. About a woman who had been murdered.' She shook her head in disgust.

'Both McAvoy and Kerry Matheson's phone records confirmed that their contact had stopped after the flowers were delivered. Except there was a new number Kerry started texting just afterwards. The first couple of messages had been deleted and were unrecoverable, but there was flirtation, a back and forth culminating in a plan to meet for 'a second chance.' Predictably enough, the messages were from an unregistered mobile, untraceable.'

The girl from behind the counter with the dreadlocks collected their empty mugs, asked if they wanted anything to eat. Amy seemed a million miles away, but Ruari shook his head, met her curious look with a brief smile.

'Untraceable that is, unless, like me, you traipsed around every corner shop in the vicinity of Alec McAvoy's chambers in Chancery Lane with a photo of him. And after only a two and a half weeks, you found a kind old lady who remembered quite clearly, even well over a year later, selling a pay-as-you-go SIM card around the time Kerry Matheson started texting the new number.'

'How could she be sure of the date months later?' Ruari asked. 'You just questioned whether or not I'm sure of the bloody time two nights ago.'

'Her granddaughter was born that day,' replied Amy. 'She'd been full of it, telling every customer, and the charming Scottish man bought a wee wooden rattle and said to pass it on with his congratulations. The police had never found out who the unregistered mobile belonged to. They accepted McAvoy's alibi, didn't see any reason to delve deeper into his movements. They didn't have the manpower to devote nearly three weeks to pounding the pavements of High Holborn from dawn to dusk like I did.

'But you're right, her testimony probably would have crumbled in court and that is why we are still here. And that's why we have to get it right this time, Ruari. Alec McAvoy is excellent at what he does. Six women have died and he is still on the loose. Do you know how rare it is for killers like him to evade capture for as long as he has? With all the technology the police have available to them nowadays, investigations like this are normally short and sharp. Think of the Ipswich murders a few years ago. Done and dusted in a couple of weeks. But McAvoy is always one step ahead of them, and so far, one step ahead of us. We have to change that Ruari. For Lorna's sake, for all of their sakes.'

◆◆◆

Cara had been working since the call from Lina Olofsson had come in at half past midnight the night before, and was about to go home for a few hours' rest when Jacob Adagbon rang from London.

'I've just been going over our file again,' he said as Cara suppressed a yawn. 'We interviewed someone Scottish. Could be a coincidence, but I don't like coincidences. I wasn't in the interview myself, though its ringing a bell now I'm looking at his statement. We traced some flowers sent to Kerry Matheson back to this guy, brought him in. He readily admitted they'd been on a date, but said he thought he'd come on a bit strong with the flowers because he never heard from her again. He was at a some posh dinner the night she was killed, so he was a bit of a dead end.'

'What was his name?' Cara asked.

'Umm… it's here somewhere. He was a lawyer if memory serves, barrister, maybe. I'll put his statement at the top of the pile, but as I say, he had an alibi and he could well still be in London for all I know.

'Here it is. Alec McAvoy.'

Cara felt a tingle shoot down her spine. 'We talked to him too,' she said. 'He had a drink with Lorna Stewart the evening before she died. He had an alibi for her time of death too, but that's a helluva coincidence.'

'It was a colleague of mine that actually interviewed him. All her notes are in the file, but I'll get her to give you a ring, shall I?'

'That would be great, thanks.'

They ended the call then, and Cara sat back in her chair, deep in thought.

She and Alec McAvoy had run into each other professionally, at drinks or conferences, for years. He was charming. He would always greet her warmly, ask after her husband, remember the story she told him about her nephew's rugby tots tournament. But now she thought about it, there was something about him that always made her just a little uneasy.

◆◆◆

Somewhere in the distance a siren sounded.

Inside the courtroom, the silence was palpable. Alec McAvoy, in his barrister's gown and wig, held up an old fashioned pocket watch that marked interminable second after interminable second with loud ticks that reverberated around the high walls of the courtroom. He was doing this for effect, Cara thought. He could have marked out the time with his phone or any number of digital timers, but Cara had to admit that every excruciating tick was doing its job.

McAvoy stood perfectly still in the middle of the room, equidistant from the jury, the defendant's box and the public gallery, which, for a case like this, was rammed with press. The defendant, handsome and clean cut in that American frat boy kind of way, was trussed up as though for a royal tea party. No neat suit could hide the coldness in his eyes, however; he watched with barely concealed impatience as McAvoy met the eyes of each juror, one by one, as the entire courtroom sat in rapt silence.

Riiiiiinnnggggg.

The shrill alarm shattered the tense hush. Several people jumped, one or two self conscious smiles were exchanged and faded quickly. McAvoy waited for silence to fall again before speaking.

'Two hundred and fifty-two seconds,' he said. 'Josh Caruso contends that he did not intend to kill his girlfriend. That it wasn't planned. That he was horrified, heartbroken, when he realised that he had choked her in a flash of anger for just a little bit too long and her life had slipped away.

'Did that,' McAvoy thundered, staring accusingly at each person present in turn. 'Feel like a flash?'

Cara had been vaguely aware that the case McAvoy was trying had stirred up quite a bit of media interest. On one hand, it was a depressingly standard question of domestic violence, but the glamour of the row of fancy New York attorneys giving the defendant reassuring looks and the unquestionable showmanship of Alec McAvoy made it front-page worthy. Good thing too, she thought, as McAvoy glanced briefly in her direction and she slumped behind the wide leather-jacketed back of the *Daily Record* reporter. The crowded courtroom suited her. If she was noticed, she could probably claim a general professional interest in the case, but for now, it was better if Alec McAvoy had no idea he was on her radar.

Safely behind the glass divider of the defendant's box, Josh Caruso tilted his head to one side as though considering McAvoy's words. Had it felt like a flash to him, Cara wondered. Was he reliving it now, remembering that feeling of omnipotence coursing through his veins, wishing he could be alone so he could close his eyes and give himself over to the memory?

'More than four minutes is, I submit to you —' McAvoy turned back to the jury. 'Enough time for Josh Caruso to have regained control. To have come to his senses and released his grip around the neck of the woman he tells us he loved. To have walked away.

'Earlier this week we heard testimony from the medical examiner who explained that Nicola Lawson will have — mercifully — lost consciousness within perhaps twenty seconds. Yet the defendant held on for a further two hundred and thirty-two. She couldn't have been struggling, she won't have been shouting at him or taunting him. To all intents and purposes she was gone already. She was unconscious, completely vulnerable in his arms. And still he held on, gripping ever tighter until her life was extinguished. Until his own daughter Eilidh was deprived of a mother, until Jackie and Pat were deprived of a daughter.'

Cara glanced over at Nicola Lawson's parents. Her father Pat, a large man in an ill fitting suit, gold chain and shaved head, gave no indication that he was aware of the tears streaming down his face as he clutched his wife's hands. Jackie's dark roots showed through her blonde hair, held back with a clip. She wore no makeup and her eyes seemed sunken into her skull with grief. She gave Pat a brief smile of support as his big body shuddered with a suppressed sob and Cara had a sudden vision of her as she was normally, done up to the nines, knocking back vodkas and holding court at the bar, her throaty laugh filling the pub as she roared at some dirty joke.

McAvoy had moved on to hammering home the prosecution's forensic case, skilfully leading the jury through a complex set of DNA matching and bruise patterns, then a convoluted insurance scam that meant Nicola Lawson was more valuable to the father of her child dead than alive.

He was excellent at his job, Cara thought. He presented the technical evidence in just enough detail to underline its substance but simply enough stated that it was easily grasped; all the time meticulously, almost insidiously, conveying to the jury that they could not let this crime go unpunished. It was manipulative. It was impressive. In fact, looking at the captivated expressions of the jury members, it occurred to Cara Boyle that Josh Caruso's innocence evaporated the minute Alec McAvoy QC took the case on.

◆◆◆

He wasn't sure if he had been asleep for hours or had just dropped off when he heard the thud against the window pane. He felt drugged, groggy, drained from the past few days. He hoped Charlie would leave him alone for a while. He just wanted to sleep.

The thud sounded again and adrenaline zipped through him. Was it someone banging on the door? Were they going to try to break in, find him, catch him, put him back in the dark place that made him forget who he was?

He got to his feet and crept gingerly from the library towards the front of the house. He was grateful for the thick layer of dust that coated the floors. It provided a perfect cushion for his ragged sannies with the holes over each big toe, and allowed him him to slink as silently as a cat.

He hesitated in the double-wide doorway of the grand living room. This room frightened him. The wind howled through the huge, gaping fireplace and it whispered things in his ears that he didn't want to hear. He had tried taking his axe to the fireplace, but still the wind howled.

The something hit the windowpane again but this time it smashed it and invaded the room, whipping up dust and cobwebs like a desert storm. He didn't jump. He watched the thing ricochet back and forth, fascinated.

It was a football.

He ran to the window and looked out. He just caught sight of the kids from next door as they scuttled towards the gap in the hedge.

'Hey!' he yelled and he heard them scream.

He grabbed the football then turned and ran as fast as he could through the hallway, the kitchen, out the back patio door and round the side of the house.

'Wait!'

The oldest kid, all gangly and awkward like his bones had grown too fast for him, was the only one brave enough to stop.

'It was an accident,' he said, though the catch in his voice belied his insolent stance.

'I've got your ball.'

'It wasn't us that broke your window.'

He looked around, surprised. The window was smashed. Oh yeah. He heard that happen.

'Can I play?' he asked.

CHAPTER 9

Thursday 13 March

Ruari had just forced himself to go for a run when Jack O'Donnell phoned. Ruari had slept with Lorna's PostIt note stuck to his bedside table and had dreamt about her again. It was a vague, unsettling dream in which she had been angry with him for something, but he didn't know what.

He'd woken up feeling an ache for her that sat thick and heavy in his chest. He could almost feel her breath against his neck as she snuggled up to him and whispered stories about her day. He could smell coconut, feel her silky hair against his lips as he kissed the top of her head.

He'd lain there as a pale sun streamed through the thin curtains, terrified to move and break the spell. Then his neighbour flushed the toilet above and Ruari realised his sheets were way overdue a wash, and that Lorna was gone.

'Alright pal?' Jack drawled. 'Kevin telt me to give you a ring.'

'Aye, did you get the — uhh, the toothbrush okay?'

'It's not a match,' Jack said.

Ruari staggered over to a bench in Kelvingrove Park, wiped the sweat from his brow. A smartly dressed middle-aged woman sat on the bench engrossed in a book. She didn't glance up as he sat down.

'The DNA?'

'Naw, it's no' a fucking tennis match, ya tube.'

'What?'

'The DNA you gave me is not a match for what we found on Kelly Gallagher. Your pal with the toothbrush is not the killer.'

'Right.'

Ruari knew his voice sounded faint. He felt winded, as though somebody had punched him in the gut.

'But I know who it is, and I don't know what you're playing at.'

'What?'

'Kevin said he telt ye tae forget Alec McAvoy, man. The guy is out running fundraisers for foster kids and climbing mountains in Africa for cancer research and you're thieving his toothbrush to see if he's a murderer? What are you on, Ruari?'

'How did you know it was his?'

'Guy's a criminal barrister. Last year sometime, one of his clients phoned him to come round, and he did, because he's a good guy. Turned out it was an active crime scene so we had to take a sample from him for exclusionary purposes.'

'Right. Aye, okay. Thanks Jack.'

'Look there is one —'

Ruari cut off the call, got up and started pounding his way along the Kelvin Walkway. He sprinted, swerving around casual park strollers and a big family group, ignoring the angry honk from a taxi when he bolted across the road that cuts through the park. He finally stopped when his legs started to give way under the bridge at Great Western Road.

In the shadows under the wide bridge he flinched at the noisy rumble of a heavy truck going by overhead. He clutched at the railing to stop himself from crumpling to the ground, staring unseeingly at the fast-moving whitewater torrenting its way through the city. His heart pounded, echoing in his ears, his lungs burned, legs trembled.

His phone buzzed. The number Lorna had scribbled on the PostIt was returning his call.

◆◆◆

Cara stood in the observation room, watching as Samira and Ricky took their seats in the claustrophobic interview room beyond. The young man who sat on the metal chair at the table tapped his foot nervously and jumped a mile when they came in. He shook his head at their offer of coffee, his eyes darting around the room. Samira announced for the tape that they were interviewing Martin Donnelly at 14:35, and Martin's eyes widened. He asked if he could have a coffee after all.

Cara's neck was aching again. She twisted her head back and forth in an effort to release the tightness, made a vague mental note to get a massage that she instantly forgot.

'When did you first hear of Lorna Stewart's death?' Samira asked when Ricky returned with the coffee and the interview began.

'Last night,' replied Martin, nodding as though to underscore the point. He had the soft, lilting accent of the Western Highlands, Cara noted. Medium height, sandy brown hair and pale blue eyes; he shifted nervously on his chair, loosened his tie a little. 'I landed at Glasgow airport late on account of the shuttle from London being delayed. The company always has a car waiting for me, but there was nobody there holding a card with my name on, so I went to the newsagents in the departure lounge to get some crisps or something. That's when I saw the headlines. I nearly died, I would have rung her today otherwise. Or texted maybe. Probably texted.'

'To see her again?'

Martin Donnelly nodded eagerly. 'Aye, Lorna was a great girl, we had a nice drink. I told her I was going abroad for a couple of weeks, but that I'd ring when I got back.'

'You went abroad with work, you said?'

He nodded again, his head bobbing wildly up and down. Cara thought that he'd end up with a neck like hers if he carried on like that. 'I'm in finance, for an oil company. We're suing one of our suppliers so I'm in Abu Dhabi for weeks at a time at the moment. It's easier than flying back and forth, but it plays havoc with your social life.'

His faint smile faded. 'She was lovely, Lorna,' he added. 'As far as I knew, anyway. We had just the one drink. I don't know very much about her, but I read a lot of crime thrillers, I know you need to know everything about her last movements and I saw her less than a week before she died. I think we got on quite well, but you never know, do you?'

'Would you be surprised if she had gone on a date with someone else?' Ricky asked, and Martin blinked.

'No,' he said finally, 'well, not from my point of view, we were hardly exclusive after one date. But —'

He hesitated, staring into space a moment as he tried to formulate the right words. 'But I would be surprised,' he said with another nod. Samira leaned forward and Martin immediately glanced off to one side, fixing his eyes on some scrawled graffiti on the wall.

'And why is that?'

Cara heard the note of impatience in Samira's voice and grimaced, though Martin didn't appear to have picked up on it.

'It took me weeks to persuade her to have a drink with me,' he said. 'I don't mean — I wasn't pushing her, she was definitely, I mean, she seemed interested, happy to chat with me. I actually live in Oban and I stay in Glasgow at the hotel where she worked through the week, so we saw each other quite often. I don't know many folk in Glasgow so it was nice to have someone to chat to here and there.

'Lorna was just — she seemed nervy, I suppose. Like a skittish horse that'd throw you and gallop for miles if a car honked behind it. Even when she agreed to a drink, she kept vetoing places to meet as too quiet or too out of the way. We finally met at a wine bar near the Trongate, and it was so rammed we could hardly hear ourselves think.'

'This was on what day?'

'The... Friday. Friday night, no wonder the place was jumping. I left for Abu Dhabi early Saturday morning.' He trailed off.

'Was there anything in particular that made you think Lorna seemed nervous when you met?'

Martin shrugged. 'We were surrounded by folk, but — she kept looking around like — I don't know,' he said with a helpless shrug. 'I don't know if she thought someone was watching us or if she was scared I would — I wouldn't ever,' he added, putting his hands up as though in surrender. 'I wouldn't do that. I was happy to take it slow, be pals if that's what she wanted. I wasn't in love with her or anything, she just seemed nice.'

Martin pulled a small plastic pack of tissues from his inside pocket and blew his nose loudly. 'Sorry, allergies,' he said.

'Did she mention anything that seemed odd to you, that might explain her behaviour?'

Martin thought a moment, then shook his head. 'I don't think so. Not specifically, anyway. She wouldn't let me see her home. I was a bit put out about that, her not trusting me to even know where she lived, but then when I saw the paper I understood why and I felt terrible.' He gave a shaky smile, his eyes faraway. 'I just can't quite believe it,' he muttered.

'What do you mean you understood why?' asked Ricky, and Martin blinked, stared at him blankly a moment.

'Well she must have been scared of someone,' he said. 'I thought it was a bit insulting at the time because I would never do anything like that, but obviously she was right to be scared. Have you got no idea who could have done it?'

◆◆◆

Ruari could see the Campsies on the horizon from the kitchen window of the pleasant, semi-detached house in Bishopbriggs. The kitchen was sunny, and Ruari thought he detected a faint scent of fresh paint.

Ruari stifled a yawn as he added milk to his tea. Adam Flannagan, the freelance journalist whose number Lorna had scribbled on the back of the PostIt note, fed his baby. The baby, in a purple onesie dotted with blue stars, kicked its legs in the high chair. Adam spooned what looked like mushy peas into its mouth and it yelped with excitement.

'I wonder when it becomes socially unacceptable to shriek when food comes at you,' Adam said. 'I feel like doing a dance of joy when the waiter brings my meal at a restaurant, but, you know, I don't dae it.'

'You should,' replied Ruari, dipping a ginger biscuit into his tea. 'I bet the chef would appreciate it.'

'Maybe I will. And when I get banned from every decent restaurant in the city and my wife chucks me, I'll know who to blame.'

Ruari grinned and Adam wiped up the green sludge the baby had spat back at him.

'So, you said on the phone you wanted to ask me about an article I wrote?'

'I'm not exactly sure, to be honest,' Ruari admitted. 'Sorry if this sounds a bit nuts. A friend of mine wrote your phone number on a note I found.'

'Oh aye?' Adam wiped the baby's chin, his frown dubious. 'Who's your friend?'

Ruari flinched. 'Was. Her name was Lorna Stewart.'

Recognition flickered in Adam's eyes. He gave Ruari a sympathetic smile. 'I read about what happened to her, man. I'm really sorry for your loss. It's terrible.'

'Did you talk to her?'

'Aye, I met her, in a coffee shop in the city centre. It was months ago, though.'

'What did she want to talk to you about?'

Adam hesitated, his eyes dubious. Then he shrugged. 'It was a story I wrote for the Bishopbriggs Herald. I'm a freelance journalist.' He gave a rueful grin, wiped the baby's chin again. 'My wife is in banking in Edinburgh, she supports us. Anyway, Lorna found a copy of the paper with my piece in it on the bus. She was looking for a project for her journalism class, so she asked me for advice on tackling this story. I didn't think it was worth her bother, to be honest, and I told her that.'

'But you don't know whether or not she took your advice?' Ruari asked.

Adam shrugged. 'I never heard from her again.'

'Have you got a copy of the article you wrote, by any chance?'

'I'll have it filed somewhere, I'll have a look,' said Adam. He scraped the last of the jar of baby food onto the spoon, then staved off the inevitable fury with a handful of Cheerios. 'It was about a murder that took place locally. The twenty-year anniversary was around then so the paper commissioned a wee piece. There wisnae much to it, to be honest,' he said. 'Only thing interesting about it was that it was never solved.'

Adam thought a moment, watching the baby content-edly munching Cheerios. 'The victim was called Elaine MacPherson.'

Ruari felt a stab of excitement as he realised that he had heard that name somewhere before. No, he'd read it.

Glasgow Ballet Murder.

'Wasn't she a nurse at Stobhill?' he asked.

'Yeah that's right. She worked at the hospital that day, then left her shift as normal according to colleagues. Her son's school raised the alarm an hour or two later because she hadn't shown up to pick him up. A search was organised, but she wasn't found until the next morning, in Robroyston Park, not far from the hospital. She'd been bashed over the head with a rock which was found nearby, but it didn't have any fingerprints or DNA, just a few wool fibres.'

'Gloves?'

Adam nodded. 'Seems so. The police unofficially concluded that it was a mugging gone wrong, even though she still had her purse and keys on her. The investigation yielded dead end after dead end. No witnesses, no evidence, nobody with a grudge against her, nothing.'

'So they just dropped it?'

Adam shrugged, topping up his tea from the pot. The baby held up a soggy Cheerio to Ruari for inspection. He gave it a distracted smile and the baby popped the Cheerio into its mouth and cackled.

'Not much they can do in a situation like that. One of the detectives I talked to, his theory was that it was one of those gang initiations where they have to kill somebody to be let in. It was all a bit frenzied and messy, and seemingly random. Coroner's report concluded she wasn't killed outright, but because she wasn't found until the following morning it was too late.'

'Was she well-hidden?'

'I'd have to double check the exact details, but she definitely wasn't buried or anything. Just on a quieter pathway, I think, and of course it was dark.'

'Didn't her family object to the investigation being dropped?'

'She didn't have much, from what I could find out. She was an only child and her parents had both died quite young, several years before. The only real mystery was how she'd ended up in the park. The police concluded that she was killed more or less where she was found, and probably that the killer panicked and ran off as soon as she was unconscious.'

The baby started to wail and Adam gave it another handful of Cheerios.

'It was a winter's afternoon so it would have been dark or nearly dark when she left work, plus she was supposed to have gone straight to pick her wee boy up, so it was strange that she apparently decided to take a walk in the park.'

Adam grinned ruefully. 'Or at least, I tried to spin it into a big mystery to have something to hang the article on.'

'There was just no sign of her ever again after she left work?'

'Bear in mind this was twenty years ago. She didn't have a mobile, even CCTV wasn't quite as prevalent back then. I think there was a camera over the hospital entrance which caught her leaving, but no others in the car park and her car was where she had left it that morning, so no traffic cameras picked her up. Colleagues reported that she hadn't received any personal calls during her shift. She just left work and disappeared.'

'I can imagine why the story caught Lorna's eye,' Ruari said. 'A woman alone in the world, left to die in a dark park on her own.' He shuddered. 'Horrible thought.'

'Right enough,' Adam signed. 'It's a dead tragic story, but I can't see what it would have to do with Lorna's murder. Some random mugger comes out of retirement all of a sudden after twenty years?' Adam shrugged. 'Listen, sorry to rush you but I need to pack this one up and get my eldest from school in a few minutes.'

◆◆◆

After all the excitement of the lab reporting they had found a microscopic speck of blood on Kelly Gallagher's neck, Cara had felt like screaming when the results from the database came back and there was no match. Without anything to compare it to, the DNA was useless. All it did was suggest that Kelly Gallagher had died at the hands of another human.

Cara stood in front of her office window, staring out at the choppy greyness of the Clyde. A low barge made its way down the river, buffeted back and forth by the wind. On the horizon, a single shard of light had broken through the clouds and was highlighting distant tower blocks in brilliant sunshine against the murky day.

'This drink with Martin wasn't in Lorna's calendar or journal, was it?' she asked, though she knew the answer. She had Lorna's last weeks memorised. She drove to and from the station every day from her home in Bearsden on automatic pilot, replaying Lorna's every movement in her head, endlessly searching for the missing link or moment that would start to untangle the investigation.

'No ma'am,' said Samira. 'According to Martin, their meeting was spontaneous in the end. He had been coming back from a long night at the office when she was finishing her shift and they decided to go then and there.'

'Seems a bit at odds with his description of her cautiousness, doesn't it?' Cara said, still staring out the window. 'To be almost obsessed with security then pop off for a drink with a strange man at the drop of a hat?'

'Well he said they had been chatting for weeks at that point,' said Ricky. 'He wasn't exactly a strange man any more. Maybe she had decided she could trust him.'

'But she hadn't mentioned him to any friends.' Cara turned around then, and looked at the photograph of Lorna that was tacked to the whiteboard in her office. The photo was from her university ID card, the only one they could find where she wasn't laughing or pulling a funny face. 'Every last one of her friends and family describes her as a force of nature, confident, headstrong. Her sister made a point of insisting Lorna was a terrible one for throwing herself headlong into things without considering the consequences. Why did she give this one guy the impression she was a quivering wreck?'

'Sometimes people show different sides of themselves to different people,' said Ricky. 'Maybe the confidence was a front with those close to her, and she didn't bother to pretend with this Martin.'

'Or maybe it was something about him that made her nervous,' Samira suggested. 'I didn't like the way he kept going on about how he didn't push her into anything. What's that saying about 'doth protest too much'? Creep.'

Cara crossed over to the whiteboard, and pulled the photo of Lorna down. She held it a moment, staring at the jumbled mass of notes and thoughts and scribbles, then stuck it up again, on the opposite side to the photos of the other victims. She circled it with a red marker, then stepped back, absentmindedly twirling the marker around her fingers like a baton.

'Did you notice when he pulled out those tissues?' Samira was saying. 'The logo on the packet was one I've never seen before, H-E-B in a red circle. I looked it up online just before we came in here and it's a supermarket chain that's only in Texas in the States and some parts of Mexico. Didn't he say he just got back from Abu Dhabi?'

'But he's in oil,' Ricky pointed out. 'Could easily have gone to Texas other times. Don't you remember that programme *Dallas*? They were rich because of oil, that was what they were all feuding about.'

Cara turned around, raised an eyebrow with a grin. Ricky shrugged with mock defensiveness. 'My mother watched it when I were a lad. I didn't pay it any attention.'

◆◆◆

The sun was long-gone from the beer garden of The Record Factory and the tip of Ruari's nose frozen by the time Greer began the story of Lorna's determination to hatch herself a pet chicken from supermarket eggs.

'She must have been seven or eight, and for months we'd suddenly start smelling this stink like you can barely imagine, somewhere about the house. We'd have a wee hunt and there would be one of Lorna's eggs, tucked under the sofa or in a gravy boat in the cabinet with the fancy china. Mum and Dad had to cut out a whole section of the living room carpet after the smell seeped so deeply into it that nothing would get it out. Then she went quiet all of a sudden and we thought she'd got bored of the notion — or accepted that eggs that come from Tesco's are unlikely to hatch. It was winter at the time, and really bad weather — loads of storms and snow that year — and so Dad couldn't take us up to our usual Saturday place in the Campsies.'

Greer started to giggle, and a few others joined in. Kerry had tears streaming down her face that she didn't bother to wipe away.

'Then finally one Saturday the weather was okay, so off we went. The whole way, during the drive, the hike up to our spot, Lorna had this wee look of the devil about her, and we should have known.' Greer laughed harder. 'The stench hit us from miles away with the wind, but for ages we couldn't find any eggs. Until finally I remembered. The summer before, we had found this wee — it's like a tiny cave really, underneath the roots of this ancient tree. We'd decided it was our fairy palace and had decorated it with twigs and bits of sheep fluff we'd found on branches and bushes, and sure enough — there it was. *Night of the Living Dead* in a nest she'd built with leaves. This pile of pure foul, rotting, rancid eggs. Lorna was inconsolable. But the worst bit was that tree had been growing for hundreds of years, and later that spring it just gave up and fell down.'

'Poor wee tree.' Kerry was sobbing openly now.

'It actually made the cave hidey hole better, because the trunk covers it now. It has seen many an illicit bottle of rum in its time I can tell you,' Greer grinned.

Ruari stared at Greer, his heart racing. A hidey hole. In the Campsies. Where Lorna's body was found.

He had never bought the idea that she had randomly decided to take a date up to the middle of nowhere in the dead of night.

The German was laughing. 'I can't believe Lorna had such a murky tree-murdering past and we never knew.'

'It's true. Ruari, back me up, you saw it the day we went up there. I pointed our den out to you.'

'What if she was hiding something there?' Ruari said.

'What?'

'Your hidey hole. What if that's why she went up there that night? Nobody in their right mind would suddenly decide to go a hike in the middle of the night. She must have taken him there or he followed her. There's no way he could have known about it otherwise.'

'The police would have found it if so,' scoffed the German and Ruari remembered that he hated him.

'Not necessarily,' he snapped. 'I do remember you pointing it out Greer, and it's a good bit away from where she was found. They would have searched for forensics over a certain radius, but not necessarily that far unless there was a particular reason to.'

'She went up there,' Greer said, staring at Ruari with wide eyes. 'That weekend before. She came out to mum and dad's and said she wanted to go a walk up there. She asked me to come but I was helping Dad repair his garden shed so she went on her own.'

Greer got up. Ruari was already on his feet. 'Let's go.'

◆◆◆

There was a feeling growing inside Alec McAvoy, but he wasn't sure what it was. It fizzed and spat and it was a struggle to keep his hands casually at his sides when all he wanted to do was shove the stupid wee guy against the wall and demand he admit he knew where Amy was.

Alec forced a smile as the lettings agent guy fumbled with a giant, jangling keyring. The letting agent frowned as he took an excruciating amount of time to decide which one to try in Amy's door next.

'We used to have a system for this,' he announced and Alec swallowed the urge to roar at him to get on with it. 'We had a wee cabinet thingmy with all the individual keys labeled, but then you'd have them all loose in your pocket and they'd get mixed up anyway, so I just went back to having them all on the one ring. They all ended up in my pocket anyway, so what was the point in —'

'They could still be labelled on the ring,' Alec snapped.

'Aye so they could,' the letting agent said, a thrilled smile lighting up his hangdog features. 'That's a good idea. No' just a pretty face, are you?'

He tried another key in the lock. It didn't fit. He whistled a tuneless song as he cheerfully went on to the next.

'Could I ask you to — it's just that she's — she's diabetic. She could have collapsed, passed out — we really can't waste any time —'

With a panicked expression, the letting agent jangled the next key in the lock with such fervour that he dropped the whole ring and spent what felt like several minutes patting around on the doormat for it. 'That's terrible, so it is. My nephew's got that, he cannae read a bloody thing.'

'I beg your pardon?'

'Naw sorry, dyslexic. He's got that dyslexic. What did you say your Amy had again?'

'Why don't I try?' Alec grabbed the keyring from the floor and started deftly working his way through it, trying key after key after key.

'I telt ye though, she just helps me out with the cleaning and that. She said she was using it as an address while she's between places.' The man watched Alec's frantic movements with a concerned frown. 'Son did you hear me? She doesn't live —'

The door clicked open with a mournful creak and Alec burst into the flat. He recoiled as a cloying smell of damp reached him, covered his nose with his hand as he charged through the empty rooms.

'Where is she?' he demanded. The flat was tiny and cramped and clearly hadn't been lived in for a very long time. Mould crept through every corner and crevice and a thick layer of dust covered the floors and windowsill.

'Ah should really get this place done up,' the letting agent commented mildly as another cloud of dust flew up as Alec charged by. 'Students would pay a decent rate if it had a lick of paint, wouldn't they?'

The stinging, suffocating feeling rose and roared through Alec McAvoy and it hit him that it was fear. Amy was missing. Without another word, he turned and clattered down the stairs, leaving the dumbfounded letting agent staring after him open mouthed.

◆◆◆

If the pathway was tricky when they'd hiked it before in murky daylight, it was treacherous in the dark. The taxi driver had been dubious about dropping them off at the end of a dirt track that led to nowhere, but Greer had disappeared into the darkness as soon as she jumped out the car. Ruari had to abandon reassuring the driver and scurry onto the path to catch up with her.

It was an unusually clear night, with only a few purple clouds dotting the sky.

'Glasgow looks like a flying saucer,' commented Greer.

Ruari looked and she was right. The orange glow of the city lights appeared to hover on the horizon like a gigantic spacecraft. 'If it turns out we're a city of visiting aliens it would explain a lot,' he replied and they both laughed more than was necessary.

Some creature screeched into the darkness and a shiver ran down Ruari's spine. He remembered the sense he'd had the last time, of Lorna dancing with the fairies she and Greer had played with as children, their whispers and giggles being scattered by the wind. Tonight it was still and the silence pounded in Ruari's ears.

The light from his phone flashlight meant Ruari could see where he was putting his feet, but it made the darkness around the tiny pool of light even deeper. He looked up suddenly, an irrational terror that Greer had disappeared clutching at him. But she was still there, hiking a few metres ahead of him, as surefooted as a mountain goat.

She suddenly yelped and Ruari's heart leapt into his mouth but then she laughed, shone her phone flashlight ahead of her to illuminate a sullen sheep staring at them. The sheep was blocking the narrow path and no amount of shouting would persuade her to scram, so they ended up scrabbling over some exposed rocks and bumming back down to the path.

'That sheep's an arsehole,' grinned Greer, though Ruari could see in the unreal glow of his phone light that her smile was tight, her eyes tense. 'Nearly there,' she muttered.

Finally they rounded the crest and the moon came out, bathing the millennia-old Roman wall in a silvery glow.

A crow squawked somewhere, and horror scuttled down Ruari's spine. He swallowed. 'Where's the hidey hole?' he asked.

'This way.' Greer's voice floated to him from the darkness. She was already scrabbling down towards the copse of trees that was silhouetted against the night sky. As Ruari followed her, he could see the outline of the ancient trunk that jutted out at a weird angle, and resisted the impulse to laugh suddenly at Lorna and her eggs.

Who'd want a chicken for a pet, anyway? He'd been pecked by one on a school trip years ago. They were grouchy wee bastards.

Greer stepped gingerly over the gnarled twists of roots and foliage. 'It's grown a bit in twenty-odd years,' she said tightly. She wobbled, and grabbed Ruari's hand to steady herself.

He propped his phone in his pocket so that the light stuck out, and carefully climbed behind her. The light streamed uselessly off to one side, but it was better than plunging them both into total darkness. The trees were slick with rain, icy cold and soft to touch.

'My arm isn't long enough,' muttered Greer. 'A big root has blocked the entrance a bit, can you get at it?'

Ruari lay down flat, vaguely noting that a stinging nettle brushed against his exposed ankle as he inched forward so as to get as close to the opening as possible. Cold beads of sweat formed on his forehead. He shone his phone flashlight around the root into the opening. It was bigger than he'd imagined, yawning deep into the hill underneath the tree. He could quite imagine wee girls scrabbling easily in and out with their treasures. Outlaws even, over the centuries, hiding from centurions or Redcoats. Until the thick root blocked the entrance, Ruari could have just about made it in himself, he thought. If he were desperate enough.

Then he saw it. A metallic glint, a flash of red, just off to the right behind a pile of stones. He lay down again, wriggled closer and felt around until his fingers closed over something smooth and metal. A box. After some more fumbling he managed to hook his finger around the handle and drag it out.

It was one of those money boxes you could pick up in any stationery shop. Red, slightly chipped. A small silver lock snapped it shut.

'Is there a key?' Greer asked.

Ruari shook his head. He leaned over to where a jagged rock stuck out of the ground and slammed the box against it. The crash echoed through the night and a few birds squawked in protest. The box wasn't totally smashed, but bent enough that, by the light of Greer's phone, they could see what was inside.

A USB stick.

◆◆◆

Alec McAvoy seemed smaller than she had realised, Cara thought. Normally he was holding court, literally or at networking drinks, his smooth chat and confident laughter giving the impression of a commanding presence. He wasn't a short man, but as Cara watched him from the observation room, sitting alone at the interview table ignoring the paper cup of tea someone had placed in front of him, she reflected that he was fairly slight, fine boned. *Like a strong wind would do him in*, her Granny would have said. *Skinny malinky long legs.* Cara thought of Lina Olofsson. Was there any possibility it was Alec McAvoy who had brushed against her and her wee dog in the dark that night?

Cara glanced up as a couple of young officers approached the interview room.

'I'll take this one,' she said suddenly, stepping forward, blocking their path.

'It's just a competent adult not been seen for a couple of days.'

'I know, but Alec McAvoy is a prominent barrister. Best give him the red carpet treatment.'

◆◆◆

'Alec,' said Cara a moment later, coming into the room. 'Sorry to see you here. Did someone get you tea okay? Or would you prefer coffee?'

He got up, shook her hand with a firm grip. His hand was cool and dry. For some reason, she shuddered.

'Thank you for talking to me.' He gave a brief smile that didn't reach his eyes, then looked away. He's uncomfortable, Cara thought. Embarrassed?

'I'm fully aware that she could just be avoiding me and if that's the case I'll — but you see the thing is, Amy — she's a bit unusual.'

'Why don't we take it one step at a time,' Cara suggested. 'How long has it been since you last saw — Amy, is her name?'

'Just over two days.'

'Do you live together?'

He shook his head. 'We've just been seeing each other a few weeks. But she hasn't been in to work either, and —'

Alec looked away again, a faint blush creeping over his features. He was hunched over, clasping his hands together, his eyes darting to and fro. Nervous energy thrummed in the air.

'The flat she told me was hers, where I've been picking her up and dropping her off for weeks, it's lying empty. Has been for months. I have no idea where she lives.'

'So you haven't visited her at home in all the time you have known one another?'

'She wanted to take things slowly.'

'You said she hasn't been at work. Have you spoken to her boss at all?'

Alec nodded. 'She covered for her to begin with, said she was home ill. Moira is a lovely lady, a bit over-protective but her heart is in the right place. I went back this morning after I discovered Amy had given me a fake address, and that's when Moira admitted she hadn't seen or heard from her either. And her phone has been cut off too, it seems.'

'What about other friends, family?'

Alec shrugged helplessly. 'None that I know of.'

Cara nodded. She doodled on her notebook, keeping it carefully out out of Alec's sight, as she thought this over.

'Alec, I hate to say this, but —'

'Yes it has occurred to me that she is married.'

Cara nodded with an apologetic smile. 'I'm sorry.'

"I don't know, I just — I can't see how, between her work and the time she spent with me, a husband could barely have seen her in all the time we've known each other. Unless he travels or works on an oil rig or something. I have thought about every possibility I can come up with.' He gave another of those odd, brief smiles, like a nervous twitch.

'Amy has always been cagey about her past,' he admitted. 'I thought I had picked up between the lines that she had escaped a bad relationship, that she was maybe even hiding from an ex-partner. I'm not certain, and especially now I'm wondering if I ever —' Alec cut himself off with a shaky breath. He looked up at Cara and she had to work not to flinch at the raw pain in his eyes. 'I don't know if I ever knew her.'

'Okay.' She nodded slowly. 'Let's take some details, the address of her home that you knew of, her work, phone number. We can take a look to see if it has been cut off at the request of the customer.' She smiled, reached over and patted his hand. 'Try not to worry too much. She could well have impulsively gone to visit a friend or something. It happens all the time.'

◆◆◆

Greer silently eased open the front door of her parents' semi-detached house on the sleepy cul-de-sac in Kirkintilloch. The front porch was filled with flowering plants, the clashing scents making Ruari feel as though he'd walked onto a tropical island. Greer put her finger over her lips.

'Watch your step,' she breathed. 'There's a creaky floorboard there — and there.' She grinned. 'Years of practice.'

A moment later they sat on the floor in the tiny, cosy living room. The walls were crammed with photos of Greer and Lorna growing up, making faces at the camera, cuddling with cousins, dancing in bridesmaid dresses. Greer put on the electric fire and its warm orange glow was comforting as they waited for her bulky, ancient laptop to fire up.

'I hope this old thing can handle whatever she saved on that,' Greer muttered. 'If not we'll have to go into town. Mum and Dad aren't exactly technophiles. We finally persuaded them to get mobiles last year and they keep them switched off the whole time to conserve their battery.'

Ruari's heart was thudding as the laptop flickered and blinked. Finally a desktop screen appeared, the background photo a teenaged Lorna and Greer with their faces smooshed together, on holiday somewhere, tanned and grinning. A hard lump formed in Ruari's throat.

Greer stuck the USB stick into the drive and opened up the file.

Lorna Stewart Blog

Lorna's blog. The missing blog he thought the police had seized. Greer started to open the first file, but Ruari pointed to the screen. 'That's a video file,' he said.

Greer clicked on it and the old laptop whirred as it struggled to open the big file, but finally, Lorna's face filled the screen. She wore earphones, and was looking down, as though writing something out of shot.

Greer clicked play and a little circle on the video whirled maddeningly round and round for several seconds, then the shot shifted to a man and Ruari realised it was a recording of some kind of web call. The man wore what looked like medical scrubs, a loose top with a V neck in a dark, blood red colour. His mop of fluffy sandy blonde hair was streaked with silver here and there. He had a small, sharp face and wore steel-rimmed glasses that gave off the impression of him being an inquisitive owl. He stared at the camera with intensely blue eyes, as though listening carefully to whatever Lorna was saying.

The wee circle whirled around and around, but an ice-cold wave of horror was slithering through Ruari.

'I know who that is,' he said. The café. Moira jabbing her finger at the mugshot in the tabloid.

I had tae put the news on mute after that lawyer said he turned his victims inside out. Didnae half give me the boak.

'It's Stuart Henderson.'

◆◆◆

Monday 3 March, 4:55pm

'I don't resent any of the things that have been done to me,' said Stuart Henderson with a deep, melancholic sigh. He peered at the camera from behind those odd wee glasses.

For a moment, his bemused expression put her in mind of the time when answering machines first became common and her Granny would leave messages consisting of her bellowing at the top of her voice *WILL YOU JUST TELL MY DAUGHTER-IN-LAW THAT GRANNY STEWART PHONED. BYYEEEE!*

Then Lorna remembered that he'd only been in prison for seven years, and had been some kind of a wonderkid developer before that. Stuart Henderson knew fine what a webcam was. But he wanted her to see him as a doddery wee man, she thought. Interesting.

'You mean things that the police did to you?' she asked.

'The police, the courts, my lawyers. A lot of the papers said they were out to get me but I don't think that was the case. I think they did their jobs as best they knew how. True, they could have done better.' He shrugged, smiled at the camera, an endearing, *don't-you-worry-about-little-old-me* smile that made Lorna's skin crawl.

'What do you think they could have done better?' she asked.

Stuart laughed, a thin, reedy laugh that jangled Lorna's nerves. Though she knew he was thousands of miles away under lock and key, an uneasy feeling kept prickling at the back of her neck. It took a superhuman effort not to run and double check that her doors were locked and that Stuart Henderson wasn't hiding under her bed.

'Well they could have caught the guy who actually did these reprehensible things,' he sing-songed, as though talking to a baby. 'Just an idea.'

'What do you think he is like?'

'Who?'

But a flicker of interest sparked into Stuart's eyes.

'The guy who actually did these reprehensible things.'

'Oh aye, him. How should I know what he's like?'

'You told me earlier that nobody knows more about this case than you do. So you should have an idea of what the real killer is like.'

'So I should,' Stuart muttered, staring up at the ceiling. He had been brought in to some kind of interview room. Lorna could just about see the dark grey walls around the edges of the shot, and every time Stuart moved his hands she heard his shackles clink and clank. After months of emails back and forth with the prison authorities and Henderson's legal team, Lorna had been thrilled to finally secure the interview. It had just been a few minutes, and she was fighting the urge not to slap her laptop shut so he couldn't see her anymore.

He wasn't what she had expected. Though she had seen plenty of pictures of him beforehand, it was still disconcerting to come face-to-face with someone who looked like any wee Glasgow guy, yet was also a monster. Lorna could have sat opposite Stuart Henderson on the subway, been cornered by him in a pub slurring rubbish chat up lines, bantered with him in a late night café as they waited for their kebabs, and she would never have known she was staring into void of humanity. He kept sniffing and she wanted to snap at him to get a hankie, then she remembered that he was chained to his chair so that he didn't rip the face off any of the guards supervising him.

'Maybe I was mistaken,' she said lightly. 'Thinking you knew all about it.'

'What do you want to know about him?' Stuart snapped, and Lorna jumped.

'Where did he start?'

Stuart rolled his eyes like a sullen teenager. 'All this is a matter of record.'

'I don't think so.'

Stuart stared at the camera. Though Lorna knew it wasn't actual eye contact, that he couldn't in fact even see her, she shivered.

'I think he must have started before the crimes we know about,' Lorna said softly. 'Long before. Killers like him, the ones who are precise and exacting and get away with it for years like he did, they don't just spring into being fully-formed. They've practiced, they've trained. They've worked their way up to it.'

Stuart nodded slowly. 'You just might be onto something there.'

'Tell me about his first crime.'

Stuart thought a long while. Lorna hardly dared breathe. Then he smiled.

'He was only a wee boy,' he grinned, as though about to spill a delicious secret.

◆◆◆

'Can you not go any faster?'

The taxi driver glanced in the rear-view mirror as the car sped along the empty M8 towards the city, and shook his head. 'Ah'm no' getting a ticket for your sake, pal, sorry.'

'It's urgent. I'm a police officer.'

'How're you no' in a police car then?'

Ruari sighed in frustration and sat back against the seat as the car finally swerved onto the slip road for Argyle Street.

'We'll get there when we get there,' Greer said quietly, staring out the window. The precious USB stick was in Ruari's jacket pocket. He kept double-checking it was there, half convinced it would evaporate at any moment.

He whacked her over the head and he ran away.

Tiny spiders of horror scuttled down Ruari's spine as he remembered the soft voice of Stuart Henderson suddenly bursting from the laptop as the picture freed up for a few seconds. He started to laugh, but was cut off by the wee circle again, his manic glee frozen on the screen. Ruari was relieved.

He whacked her over the head and he ran away.

The USB stick seemed almost malevolent itself, as though Ruari was holding the darkness of Stuart Henderson in his pocket. His stomach turned and he willed the taxi to reach the police station faster.

◆◆◆

'Cara Boyle. DCI Cara Boyle. It's urgent we speak to her personally right away.' The uniformed officer who was manning the front desk regarded Ruari and Greer with a patient look. He was nearing retirement age, with thick bushy eyebrows that reminded Ruari of McAvoy's security guard.

'What's your name, son?'

'It's about Lorna Stewart. Please could you contact her or someone on her team.'

The front desk officer picked up the phone with maddening slowness. 'I have crucial information about Lorna Stewart's murder. Please.'

'Isn't that her?' said Greer.

Cara Boyle was walking down the corridor towards them.

'DCI Boyle?' Ruari had blurted her name out before he clocked that she was with Alec McAvoy. 'I need to show you something, urgently.'

'Ruari MacCallan isn't it? A friend of Lorna Stewart's. And you're her sister.'

Ruari glanced at McAvoy, but his expression didn't betray a thing.

'We found this. It's Lorna's. There is saved on it a video on it that Lorna made of a web call with Stuart Henderson from prison. He confessed to a murder from twenty years ago in Glasgow. There's several posts she had written as well. Lorna was investigating this cold case for her blog and then she managed to get an interview with Henderson.'

'Stuart Henderson the serial killer?' asked Cara in confusion.

Ruari nodded, handed the USB stick over to Cara who looked at it as though it might explode. 'He can't have killed Lorna obviously, but —' He jabbed his finger urgently at the stick in Cara's hands. 'She hid it. Up in the Campsies were she was found — where her killer found her.'

'Okay. Alec, I need to deal with this. We'll talk again tomorrow, okay?'

'Who was the victim?' Alec McAvoy blurted, his voice tight.

'I don't think —' Cara began.

'Please. Who was it?'

'Her name was Elaine MacPherson,' Ruari said. 'I don't know if —'

Alec visibly blanched, staggered back half a step as though he'd been shoved.

'Alec?' said Boyle.

'I always thought —' he muttered, a dazed look in his eyes. He stared frantically at Boyle. 'Elaine MacPherson was my mother.'

It took Ruari a moment to realise that the strangled, choking sound filling the reception was Alec McAvoy crying.

CHAPTER 10

Friday 14 March

Cara Boyle had promised to follow up with Ruari and Greer first thing in the morning, as soon as she and her team had had a chance to properly review Lorna's video. She advised them to try to get some sleep, but they both knew it was impossible. They had found themselves in a 24-hour McDonalds, splitting a mountain of fries they barely tasted.

A crowd of rowdy construction workers came in to order breakfast and Ruari blinked when he saw it was daylight outside. Greer said she had better get to her parents' to update them, and he walked her out to the car park where she flagged down a taxi. Ruari trudged home, checking and double-checking his phone every minute for news from Boyle.

The concept of sleep seemed a distant memory as Ruari paced his tiny, claustrophobic flat. He made some instant coffee with three heaped tablespoons of granules. He flicked the TV on and off again, scrolled through his phone. As the whitewater of adrenaline finally started to subside, he belatedly noticed that he had also smashed up his hand when he slammed the money box into the rock. It was throbbing with pain, his knuckles torn and bleeding. He absentmindedly wrapped it in a dish towel that had seen better days, opened up his laptop and typed *Stuart Henderson* one-handed.

Henderson's crimes were truly horrifying. He had been convicted of murdering seventeen women across Texas, Arkansas, Mississippi and Lousiana, although police speculated there were as many as ten more they couldn't charge him with. The sheer gore of his murders was macabre, theatrical even, and his trial had dominated the American news for months. Half way through his trial he had lost it one day, out of nowhere. He leapt over the defence table like a wild animal and lunged ferociously for one of the jurors. He was tackled to the ground by several huge bailiffs, and given a sedation shot in full view of the news cameras. He spent the rest of the trial chained to his chair.

He had been convicted and sentenced to death just over six years previously, and the most recent article Ruari could find announced that his execution was scheduled for three months' time. The newly elected state governor had announced a crackdown on interminable death row waits. Ruari opened up a video interview, listened as the governor drawled to a cheering crowd that once an inmate was sentenced there was no reason to delay sending him to hell.

The video cut to a shot of Henderson being led from the courtroom to a waiting prison van, and Ruari shuddered. He looked wee and rodent-like, a rabbit caught in headlights, yet it was like looking into a void of humanity. A monster in human form. A living nightmare. And Lorna had talked to him.

Purposefully shutting down the video, Ruari winced as his bad hand protested, and typed with his left hand *Stuart Henderson Glasgow.*

Halfway down the page was a hit that sent Ruari's heart plummeting and he felt a tremble from deep within, like an earthquake in his guts.

He should have known.

How could he not have known?

A photo filled the screen, of a smiling, younger Stuart, grinning happily into the camera in a charcoal grey suit, his arm firmly around the waist of his bride in a simple dress of a style from around a decade ago. Her long, startlingly red hair was whipped up by the wind.

Bishopbriggs Registry Office: Stuart Andrew Henderson marries Amy Charlotte Kerr.

◆◆◆

'The sheer scale of it was like something out of a film, I mean *thirty-seven* bodies, not to mention all the bizarre things he had done to them. It was so far beyond horrific that you just couldn't tear your eyes away.'

Cara loved to watch Stellan cook. He was so precise, measuring exactly this spice or that as opposed to the random, optimistic dashes of whatever caught her eye that she favoured. The kitchen filled up with mouthwatering smells, and Cara sipped a full-bodied red and smiled at Stellan's frown as he levelled off half a teaspoon of curry powder. Her team had spent the day going over the investigation into Elaine MacPherson's murder, and had failed to come up with a single connection between it, the London murders, and the three recent Glasgow victims.

Except Alec McAvoy. He was Elaine MacPherson's son, and had been on dates with Kerry Matheson and Lorna Stewart. Yet he had alibis for all three murders. That afternoon, he had willingly given a DNA sample which the lab, with impressive speed, ruled out as a match for that which they had found on Kelly Gallagher's body. Cara didn't believe in coincidences. Alec MacAvoy had to be, somehow, the key to all of it, but she was damned if she could think of how.

'Yeah I remember it being on the news in Sweden too,' Stellan said, tasting the sauce with a critical frown. 'More ginger, I think.'

'Really? I wouldn't have expected Sweden to care.'

'We love anything that is American and shocking,' he said with a shrug, tossing another half a teaspoon of ground ginger in and setting the sauce on a low heat to simmer. He went to the fridge and got out a couple of chicken breasts, sliced them up expertly. 'And we quite like Scottish things too.'

'I was fascinated by his wife,' Cara said. 'One of the American news sites did a live stream of the trial, and a few of my friends would sit up every night watching it. We had a drinking game for it.' Cara shook her head, remembering. 'There was something about the way she sat there, right behind the defense table, totally stoic, not showing any emotion whatsoever. I swear some of the papers were harder on her than on him. She must have known, she drove him to it, she was the real evil mind and he was just a puppet.'

Stellan shook his head, browning the chicken lightly in a frowning pan. 'That is impressive misogyny,' he commented. 'A man tears thirty-seven women apart and it is all his wife's fault.'

'Exactly,' said Cara, with a laugh. She hopped down from the counter to grab the wine bottle, standing on tiptoes to kiss the nape of Stellan's neck as she passed.

'I went to a talk at Stockholm University some years ago by a man who runs a group called The Four Percent,' he said, pouring the sauce over the browned chicken bits.

'I think I've heard of them — they're anti death penalty, aren't they?' Cara topped up her wine, and reluctantly decided that had better be it for the evening. A night off would do her productivity the world of good, but Charlie might have other plans for her.

'Yes that's right. I am too. When you think of even a man like this Henderson walking, all shackled and chained up, into a room to be strapped to a gurney from which he will never get up, it is *yust* barbaric. I'm not saying he deserves mercy, but it's mediaeval.'

Stellan dished the rice into a bowl, and Cara had to admit that how particular he was at measuring out the water so it cooked perfectly away leaving the rice impeccably fluffy, was impressive.

'My main issue with it is that it doesn't work as a deterrent, so all that it achieves is to satisfy blood lust,' she said. Stellan pulled up a stool next to hers and they dished up and split the naan bread with companionable ease.

'Yes, but what I want to say is, this man talked about Stuart Henderson. He believed he was innocent.'

Cara shook her head. 'I would be astounded if that was the case.'

'Maybe. But his argument was that the trial was so hyped with the media going crazy about how terrible the crimes were that it was impossible for Henderson to get a fair trial. Also he thought that the defense was lazy, all about showmanship to the cameras rather than truly serving their client. That was the gist of it as I remember, anyway.'

'I'd have to read the details again to be certain, but even if the quality of law practiced at the trial left something to be desired, the idea of him being innocent is unfathomable.'

'You look tired,' said Stellan. He reached out and massaged the back of her neck briefly. Cara caught his hand in hers and kissed his palm. 'This is our *fredagsmys*. Let's talk about something else.

'Friday night.' Cara stared at him. There had been a tiny niggle of something not quite adding up bothering her since the day before, and that was it. The Friday before Lorna Stewart died, she had been with her journalism class. They did a presentation of their week's work at the end of the week, and followed it with welcoming-in-the-weekend drinks. Several people had commented in their statements that Lorna hadn't presented that week, but they were all quite certain she was there for the whole evening.

So Lorna was not doing a shift at the hotel then going for a drink with a man named Martin.

'Shit.' Cara leaped down from her counter stool and ran to the hallway where she had left her bag. 'I'm sorry.'

Stellan waved away her apology and Cara sat cross legged on the floor by the front door, opened up her tablet and double checked the statements made by Lorna's journalism classmates and also Martin's. She was right. Martin Donnelly definitely stated Friday night, and even specified that he flew to Abu Dhabi the following morn-ing. Cara texted Samira to ask she confirm with the airline that Martin Donnelly was in fact on that flight on the Saturday morning.

◆◆◆

Samira called back just as Cara was clearing the table and banishing Stellan from helping her with the dishes.

'A Martin Donnelly was on the flight to Abu Dhabi, but I managed to track down a woman in HR for his work anyway, just to confirm the dates he had given us. She mentioned in passing that he's away this week, visiting his parents in Dublin.'

'Dublin? He told us he was from Oban.'

'Exactly. I've just texted the photo she sent me from his work ID'

Cara put the call on speaker, clicked to open the attachment, and there was Martin Donnelly. Thick black curly hair, dark flashing eyes. *Black Irish,* thought Cara dully. Allegedly the descendants of shipwrecked survivors of the Spanish Armada. And most certainly not the man who had come in to self-report meeting Lorna Stewart the Friday before she died.

◆◆◆

'Where's Amy?'

Ruari charged into the café to find Moira serving alongside the hipstery guy with the glasses again. She looked up, and he saw guilt flash into her eyes.

'She's no' well,' Moira said before Ruari opened his mouth. 'Some kind of lurgy. She's full of it.'

'Where is she?'

'Home. What's it to you, Ruari?'

Ruari held up his phone. 'I've been phoning her for the last quarter of an hour and her number is cut off.'

'That cannae be right.' But Ruari saw doubt flicker into her eyes.

'Have you spoken to her?'

Moira hesitated, then set her mouth in a thin, determined line. 'I've been round. I took her some soup. Ruari, it's none of your business, leave her —'

'You've been round to the address you gave me, the one that was on her employment application?'

'Of course. Ruari, you need to —'

'She doesn't bloody live there, Moira.'

◆◆◆

Fifteen minutes later, he paid the entry fee at the community hall and pushed his way towards the dance floor, scanning the crowd for any sign of Amy. All of a sudden the hall was plunged into darkness, and a single, silvery spotlight illuminated Taylor in his usual tracksuit and gold chain, and a woman in a long, crimson tea dress in the centre of the dance floor.

Sultry thirties blues music crackled through the speakers. With a flick of his wrist, Taylor spun the woman in to cling to his body, then dipped her low. Her long dark hair brushed along the dusty floor. A few people whooped and wolf whistled as they danced, and Ruari felt as though he had walked into another dimension.

When the music came to an end, Taylor fist bumped with the woman as the crowd whooped and cheered them. The main lights went on and the dance floor filled up as *It Ain't What You Do It's the Way That You Do It* filled the air.

'Alright Ruari man, good tae see ya again.'

'Was that your — girlfriend?'

Taylor burst out laughing. 'Must be jokin' man, Mhari's got three weans, her eldest was in my class at school though I 'hink he's in jail now. Nah, we're dance partners. We've made it through tae the swing dance championships in London next month. That's our blues number. Dead sexy is it not?' Taylor grinned lasciviously and swung his hips in an adorably comical shagging parody that made Ruari realise her was even younger than he'd thought.

'Championships, eh? That's no' bad.'

'Aye, it's smashing. First prize is a grand, man, 'magine a whole grand. I'm gonnae have a bath in it if I get it. Mhari's smashin', will I ask her if she'll give you a dance?'

'Maybe another time. Listen Taylor, have you seen Amy lately? She's not been at work a few days.'

Taylor shook his head. "Naw man, I've no'. She okay?'

'How do you mean 'okay'?'

Taylor shrugged. 'Dunno pal, she's just been a bit funny lately. She's no' been right since Lorna died.'

Spiders of horror scuttled over Ruari's neck. 'Lorna? What do you mean?'

'You were pals with Lorna too, were you not? You must've known Amy then, they were thick as thieves.'

◆◆◆

'Ma'am?' Jack O'Donnell pushed Cara Boyle's office door open, and Cara, Samira and Ricky looked up from their intense discussion. 'Sorry to interrupt —'

'It's fine, come in. You're from the lab, aren't you? What's your name again?'

'Jack O'Donnell, ma'am.' Jack's palms were sweating. Sneaking evidence into a lab, potentially contaminating everything else that was being processed, was a sackable offence and possibly a criminal one. He forced a smile he suspected looked manic, told himself that he didn't have a choice.

'I did a favour to a pal, well, a pal of my partner's but that doesnae — you're probably gonnae sack me, but just hear me out first.'

'Come in, O'Donnell' Cara said. 'Let's hear what you have to say before I decide whether or not you're sacked.'

'I'll explain how it all came about in a minute,' Jack said, and his voice sounded high and reedy in his own ears. 'But first — do any of yous know if Alec McAvoy has a brother?'

◆◆◆

Ruari stole across the moss covered patio, and without hesitation, pushed the cracked glass door open and slipped inside. The creak as the door opened reverberated in his ears and he knew that he would have alerted anyone within to his presence. But he didn't care.

The kitchen was huge, with dark beams crossing the ceiling and an enormous, gaping fireplace of dark, heavy oak. Set deep inside it was an old fashioned stove that must have once gleamed black and white but was now rusted and covered in a thick layer of gray dust. A copper kettle sat on the hob, crusted with decades of grime. As Ruari stepped into the main hallway, he disturbed a cloud of flies that flittered with eerie silence around the kitchen. The kitchen and the walls of the hallway were covered in a dark, twisting vine. Ruari couldn't be sure whether it had once been a tame houseplant left to go feral or if the ivy from outside had invaded.

Ruari paused, his feet sinking into the thick layer of dust, and listened.

There was a drip coming from somewhere, a creak or two as the old house shifted and settled. But after several minutes he had detected no indication of another human present. He felt safe enough to pull out his phone and put the flashlight on.

The hallway was dominated by a gigantic portrait, at least as tall as Ruari. It was of Alec McAvoy, Ruari thought, his heart leaping into his mouth. Then he looked at it again and realised it wasn't quite Alec, though the resemblance was startling. The nose was a little wider, hairline higher, and the man in the portrait wore a military uniform that reminded Ruari of black and white wartime films.

The brass placard was half hidden under a thick grime, Ruari could just make out *Angus, Laird...* and *1942*.

His father? Or grandfather? This man would have been in his fifties or so when Alec was born. The absent father who had set the dogs on Elaine MacPherson?

There was a creak from behind and Ruari whirled around in terror but no one was there. Had it been the patio door? He froze, his heart thudding in his ears. Somewhere in the distance he could hear the kids from next door shouting to each other as they played football in the garden. The door creaked again and he remembered it was the wind.

Someone has been living here, Ruari thought as he crept into what appeared to be a library. Several more portraits of the man who looked so like McAvoy adorned the walls, Ruari half grinned as he thought of Taylor's words that Alec didn't half fancy himself. In front the ornately carved fireplace the dust had been disturbed. A filthy sleeping bag was draped over a large walnut desk and even in the dim light Ruari could see the cloud of flies dancing over it. Around the fireplace various wrappers had been discarded. Crisps. Mars Bars. Several wine bottles, fizzy drink cans, a clear bottle of some unbranded gin was upended into the fireplace.

As Ruari stood, taking it all in, one of the fizzy drink cans rolled from the desk and clattered onto the floor.

Instinctively, he crouched and picked it up, set it back where it had been next to the sleeping bag. A glint caught his eye and he picked up the silver necklace that had been half-hidden under the sleeping bag. Chills darted through him as he held it up to the dim light near the dirt-encrusted window. It was pretty, but nothing special. No family heirloom or cherished eighteenth-birthday present. It was of a chunky silver-esque metal, set with deep turquoise imitation stones. He was fairly sure it had come from a market stall somewhere in Greece.

Lorna wore it occasionally, but not so often that anyone thought to check if it was missing. She had dozens like it.

She joked that she was a magpie, but a tight magpie who didn't trust herself not to lose pricey jewellery.

A burning bile rose in Ruari's throat as he turned the necklace over in his hands, remembering seeing it catch the light at the restaurant as Lorna laughed at something Alec McAvoy said.

He heard a floorboard creak behind him and he knew that he wasn't alone. Lorna's killer was watching him. He was cornered, trapped in a room with one doorway and somebody was standing in that doorway.

Ruari turned and just caught a glimpse of the person watching him before the rotting floorboards gave way, plunging him in to the yawning blackness of the cellar below.

◆◆◆

The pain was excruciating. It clanged through Ruari's every nerve as black spots danced in front of his eyes. Even in the darkness of the cellar, he could just spot the sickening white of a bone protruding from his left shin before a wave of dizziness forced him to slump back onto the mouldy and filthy floor.

His phone had scattered somewhere into the shadows as he fell, he heard it clatter but couldn't move to feel for it without bringing a fresh wave of white-hot agony crashing down over him.

'Amy,' he yelled. 'Please Amy — don't leave me here.'

For a moment he thought he saw her standing at the top of the rotting hole he had fallen into. Then he blinked and she was gone and a tidal wave of blackness rushed up to meet him.

END EPISODE ONE

LETTER FROM THE AUTHOR

I hope that's you I can hear yelling 'Whhaaaattt? THAT CAN'T BE THE END!!' because otherwise one of my neighbours has some problems.

The good news is, Dark of Night: Episode Two (and Three!) are out now!

Plus, if you're interested in all manner of bonus content and chat, just head over to the imaginatively titled I've Read Dark of Night Facebook Group. I'm at @csduffy-writer on Instagram, Facebook and Twitter if you'd like to say hi - I'd love to hear from you!

As you might know, reviews are vital to an indie author. If you wouldn't mind popping a wee review on Amazon, I would be ever so grateful and think nice things about you for several minutes at least :-)

Thanks a million, and looking forward to chatting with you soon!

Claire

claire@csduffy.com

xxx

www.csduffy.com

ABOUT THE AUTHOR

C.S. Duffy writes psychological suspense thrillers with a healthy dose of black humour. Her background is in film and TV. She has several projects in development in Sweden and the UK, including the feature film *Guilty*. She is the author of *Life is Swede,* a thriller that was originally written as a blog - leading several readers to contact Swedish news agencies asking them why they hadn't reported the murder that features in the blog. *Dark of Night* is her first novel.

www.csduffy.com

Lightning Source UK Ltd.
Milton Keynes UK
UKHW01f1445181018
330774UK00001B/28/P